THE GIVERS AND OTHER STORIES

MORE WILDSIDE CLASSICS

Please see www.wildsidepress.com for a complete list!

THE GIVERS AND OTHER STORIES

MARY E. WILKINS FREEMAN

WILDSIDE PRESS

THE GIVERS AND OTHER STORIES

This edition published 2005 by Wildside Press, LLC.
www.wildsidepress.com

CONTENTS

THE GIVERS

The level of new snow in Sophia Lane's north yard was broken by horse's tracks and the marks of sleigh-runners. Sophia's second cousin, Mrs. Adoniram Cutting, her married daughter Abby Dodd, and unmarried daughter Eunice had driven over from Addison, and put up their horse and sleigh in Sophia's clean, unused barn.

When Sophia had heard the sleigh-bells she had peered eagerly out of the window of the sitting-room and dropped her sewing. "Here's Ellen and Abby and Eunice," she cried, "and they've brought you some wedding-presents. Flora Bell, you put the shawl over your head, and go out through the shed and open the barn. I'll tell them to drive right in."

With that the girl and the woman scuttled — Flora Bell through the house and shed to the barn which joined it; Sophia, to the front door of the house, which she pushed open with some difficulty on account of the banked snow. Then she called to the women in the sleigh, which had stopped at the entrance to the north yard: "Drive right in — drive right in. Flora has gone to open the barn-doors. She'll be there by the time you get there."

Then Sophia ran through the house to the kitchen, set the tea-kettle forward, and measured some tea into the teapot. She moved with the greatest swiftness, as if the tea in so many seconds were a vital necessity. When the guests came in from the barn she greeted them breathlessly. "Go right into the sittin'-room," said she. "Flora, you take their things and put them on the bedroom bed. Set right down by the stove and get warm, and the tea 'll be ready in a minute. The water's 'most boilin'. You must be 'most froze." The three women, who were shapeless bundles from their wraps, moved clumsily into the sitting-room as before a spanking breeze of will. Flora followed them; she moved more slowly than her aunt, who was a miracle of nervous speed. Sophia Lane never walked; she ran to all her duties and pleasures as if she were racing against time. She hastened the boiling of the teakettle — she poked the fire; she thrust light slivers of wood into the stove. When the water boiled she made the tea with a rush, and carried the tray with cups and saucers into the sitting-room with a perilous side-wise tilt and flirt. But nothing was spilled. It was very seldom that Sophia came to grief through her haste.

The three women had their wraps removed, and were sitting around the stove. The eldest, Mrs. Ellen Cutting — a stout woman with a handsome face reddened with cold — spoke when Sophia entered.

"Land! if you haven't gone and made hot tea!" said she.

Sophia set the tray down with a jerk, and the cups hopped in their saucers. "Well, I guess you need some," said she, speaking as fast as she moved. "It's a bitter day; you must be froze."

"Yes, it is awful cold," assented Abby Dodd, the married daughter, "but I told mother and Eunice we'd got to come to-day, whether or no. I was bound we should get over here before the wedding."

"Look at Flora blush!" giggled Eunice, the youngest and the unmarried daughter.

Indeed, Flora Bell, who was not pretty, but tall and slender and graceful, was a deep pink all over her delicate face to the roots of her fair hair.

"You wait till your turn comes, Sis, and see what you'll do," said Abby Dodd, who resembled her mother, being fat and pink and white, with a dumpy, slightly round-shouldered figure in a pink flannel shirt-waist frilled with lace. All the new-comers were well dressed, the youngest daughter especially. They had a prosperous air, and they made Sophia's small and frugal sitting-room seem more contracted than usual. Both Sophia and her niece were dressed in garments which the visitors would characterize later among themselves, with a certain scorn tinctured with pity, as "fadged up." They were not shabby, they were not exactly poor, but they were painfully and futilely aspiring. "If only they would not trim quite so much," Eunice Cutting said later. But Sophia dearly loved trimming; and as for Flora, she loved whatever her aunt Sophia did. Sophia had adopted her when her parents died, when she was a baby, and had brought her up on a pittance a year. Flora was to be married to Herbert Bennet on the next day but one. She was hurrying her bridal preparations, and she was in a sort of delirium of triumph, of pride, of happiness and timidity. She was the centre of attention to-day. The visitors' eyes were all upon her with a half-kindly, half-humorous curiosity.

On the lounge at the side of the room opposite the stove were three packages, beautifully done up in white paper and tied with red and green ribbons. Sophia had spied them the moment she entered the room.

The guests comfortably sipped their tea.

"Is it sweet enough?" asked Sophia of Mrs. Cutting, thrusting the white sugar-bowl at her.

"Plenty," replied Mrs. Cutting. "This tea does go right to the spot. I did get chilled."

"I thought you would."

"Yes, and I don't like to, especially since it is just a year ago since I had pneumonia, but Abby thought we must come to-day, and I thought so myself. I thought we wanted to have one more look at Flora before she was a bride."

"Flora's got to go out now to try on her weddin'-dress the last time," said Sophia. "Miss Beals has been awful hurried at the last minute; she don't turn off work very fast, and the dress won't be done till to-night; but everything else is finished."

"I suppose you've had a lot of presents, Flora?" said Abby Dodd.

"Quite a lot," replied Flora, blushing.

"Yes, she's had some real nice presents, and two or three that ain't quite so nice," said Sophia, "but I guess those can be changed."

Mrs. Cutting glanced at the packages on the sofa with an air of confidence and pride. "We have brought over some little things," said she. "Adoniram and I give one, and Abby and Eunice each one. I hope you'll like them, Flora."

Flora was very rosy; she smiled with a charming effect, as if she were timid before her own delight. "Thank you," she murmured. "I know they are lovely."

"Do go and open them, Flora," said Eunice. "See if you have any other presents like them."

"Yes, open them, Flora," said Mrs. Cutting, with pleasant patronage.

Flora made an eager little movement toward the presents, then she looked wistfully at her aunt Sophia.

Sophia was smiling with a little reserve. "Yes, go and open them, Flora," said she; "then bring out your other presents and show them."

Flora's drab skirt and purple ruffles swayed gracefully across the room; she gathered up the packages in her slender arms, and brought them over to the table between the windows, where her aunt sat. Flora began untying the red and green ribbons, while the visitors looked on with joyful and smiling importance. On one package was marked, "Flora, with all best wishes for her future happiness, from Mr. and Mrs. Adoniram Cutting."

"That is ours," said Mrs. Cutting.

Flora took off the white paper, and a nice white box was revealed. She removed the lid and took out a mass of crumpled tissue-paper. At last she drew forth the present. It was in three pieces. When she had set them on the table, she viewed them with admiration but bewilderment. She looked from one to the other, smiling vaguely.

Abby Dodd laughed. "Why, she doesn't know how to put them together!" said she. She went to the table and quickly adjusted the different parts of the present. "There!" said she, triumphantly.

"What a beautiful — teakettle!" said Flora, but still in a bewildered fashion.

Sophia was regarding it with an odd expression. "What is it?" she asked, shortly.

"Why, Sophia," cried Mrs. Cutting, "don't you know? It is an afternoon-tea kettle."

"What's that thing under it?" asked Sophia.

"Why, that's the alcohol-lamp. It swings on that little frame over the lamp and heats the water. I thought it would be so nice for her."

"It's beautiful," said Flora.

Sophia said nothing.

"It is real silver; it isn't plated," said Mrs. Cutting, in a slightly grieved tone.

"It is beautiful," Flora murmured again, but Sophia said nothing.

Flora began opening another package. It was quite bulky. It was marked, "Flora, with best wishes for a life of love and happiness, from Abby Dodd."

"Be careful," charged Abby Dodd. "It's glass."

Flora removed the paper gingerly. The present was rolled in tissue-paper.

"What beautiful dishes!" said she, but her voice was again slightly bewildered.

Sophia looked at the present with considerable interest. "What be the bowls for?" said she. "Oatmeal?"

The visitors all laughed.

"Oatmeal!" cried Abby. "Why, they are finger-bowls!"

"Finger-bowls?" repeated Sophia, with a plainly hostile air.

"Yes, — bowls to dip your fingers in after dinner," said Abby.

"What for?" asked Sophia.

"Why, to — to wash them."

"We wash our hands in the wash-basin in the kitchen with good hot water and soap," said Sophia.

"Oh, but these are not really to wash the hands in — just to dabble the fingers in," said Eunice, still giggling. "It's the style.

You have them in little plates with doilies and pass them around after dinner."

"They are real pretty," said Flora.

Sophia said nothing.

"They are real cut glass," said Mrs. Cutting.

Flora turned to the third package, that was small and flat and exceedingly dainty. The red-and-green ribbon was tied in a charming bow, with Eunice's visiting-card. On the back of the card was written, "Flora, with dearest love, and wishes for a life of happiness, from Eunice." Flora removed the ribbons and the white paper, and opened a flat, white box, disclosing six dainty squares of linen embroidered with violets.

"What lovely mats!" said she.

"They are finger-bowl doilies," said Eunice, radiantly.

"To set the bowls on?" said Flora.

"Yes; you use pretty plates, put a doily in each plate, and then the finger-bowl on the doily."

"They are lovely," said Flora.

Sophia said nothing.

Abby looked rather aggrievedly at Sophia. "Eunice and I thought Flora would like them as well as anything we could give her," said she.

"They are lovely," Flora said again.

"You haven't any like them, have you?" Abby asked, rather uneasily.

"No, she hasn't," answered Sophia, for her niece.

"We tried to think of some things that everybody else wouldn't give her," said Mrs. Cutting.

"Yes, you have," Sophia answered, dryly.

"They are all beautiful," said Flora, in a soft, anxiously deprecating voice, as she gathered up the presents. "I keep my presents in the parlor," she remarked further. "I guess I'll put these in there with the rest."

Presently she returned, bringing a large box; she set it down and returned for another. They were large suit-boxes. She placed them on the table, and the visitors gathered round.

"I've had beautiful presents," said Flora.

"Yes, she has had *some* pretty nice presents," assented Sophia. "Most of them are real nice."

Flora stood beside the table and lifted tenderly from the box one wedding-gift after another. She was full of shy pride. The visitors admired everything. When Flora had displayed the contents of the two boxes, she brought out a large picture in an ornate gilt frame, and finally wheeled through the door with difficulty a patent rocker upholstered with red, crushed plush.

"That's from some of his folks," said Sophia. "I call it a handsome present."

"I'm going to have a table from his aunt Jane," remarked Flora.

"Sit down in that chair and see how easy it is," said Sophia, imperatively, to Mrs. Cutting, who obeyed meekly, although the crushed plush was so icy cold from its sojourn in the parlor that it seemed to embrace her with deadly arms and made her have visions of pneumonia.

"It's as easy a chair as I ever sat in," she said, rising hastily.

"Leave it out here and let her set in it while she is here," said Sophia; and Mrs. Cutting sank back into the chair, although she did ask for a little shawl for her shoulders.

Mrs. Cutting had always had a wholesome respect for her cousin Sophia Lane, although she had a certain feeling of superiority by reason of her wealth. Even while she looked about Sophia's poor little sitting-room and recalled her own fine parlors, she had a sense that Sophia was throned on such mental heights above mahogany and plush and tapestry that she could not touch her with a finger of petty scorn even if she wished.

After Flora had displayed her presents and carried them back to the parlor, she excused herself and went to the dressmaker's to try on her wedding-dress.

After Flora had gone out of the yard, looking abnormally stout with the gay plaid shawl over the coat and her head rolled in a thick, old, worsted hood of Sophia's, Mrs. Cutting opened on a subject about which she was exceedingly curious.

"I'm real sorry we can't have a glimpse of the wedding-dress," said she, ingratiatingly.

Sophia gave an odd sort of grunt in response. Sophia always gave utterance to that nondescript sound, which was neither assent nor dissent, but open to almost any interpretation, when she wished to evade a lie. She was in reality very glad that the wedding-dress was not on exhibition. She thought it much better that it should not be seen in its full glory until the wedding-day.

"Flora has got many good presents," said Sophia, "and a few tomfool ones, thanks to me and what I did last Christmas."

"What do you mean, Sophia?" asked Mrs. Cutting.

"Didn't you hear what I did, Ellen Cutting?"

"No, I didn't hear a word about it."

"Well, I didn't know but somebody might have told. I wasn't a mite ashamed of it, and I ain't now. I'd do the same thing over again if it was necessary, but I guess it won't be; I guess they got a good lesson. I dare say they were kind of huffy at the time. I guess they got over it. They've all give Flora presents now, anyhow, except Angeline White, and I guess she will."

"Why, what did you do?" asked Abby Dodd, with round eyes of interest on Sophia.

"Why, I'd jest as soon tell you as not," replied Sophia. "I've got some cake in the oven. Jest let me take a peek at that first."

"Wedding-cake?" asked Eunice, as Sophia ran out of the room.

"Land, no!" she called back. "That was made six weeks ago. Weddin'-cake wouldn't be worth anything baked now."

"Eunice, didn't you know better than that?" cried her mother.

"It's white cake," Sophia's explanatory voice came from the kitchen, whence sweet odors floated into the room. The oven door opened and shut with an exceedingly swift click like a pistol-shot.

"I should think she'd make the cake fall, slamming the oven door like that," murmured Abby Dodd.

"So should I; but it won't," assented her mother. "I never knew Sophia to fail with her cake."

Sophia flew back into the sitting-room and plumped into her chair; she had, indeed, risen with such impetus and been so quick that the chair had not ceased rocking since she left it. "It's done," said she; "I took it out. I'll let it stand in the pan and steam a while before I do anything more with it. Now I'll tell you what I did about Flora's Christmas presents last year if you want me to. I'd jest as soon as not. If I hadn't done what I did, there wouldn't have been any weddin' this winter, I can tell you that."

"You don't say so!" cried Mrs. Cutting, and the others stared.

"No, there wouldn't. You know, Herbert and Flora have been goin' together three years this December. Well, they'd have been goin' together three years more, and I don't know but they'd been goin' together till doomsday, if I hadn't taken matters into my own hand. I ain't never been married myself, and maybe folks think I ain't any right to my opinion, but I've always said I didn't approve of young folks goin' together so long unless they get married. When they're married, and any little thing comes up that one or the other don't think quite so nice, why, they put up with it, and make the best of it, and kind of belittle that and make more of the things that they do like. But when they ain't married it's different. I don't care how much they think of each other, something may come up to make him or her kind of wonder if t'other is good enough to marry, after all. Well, nothin' of that kind has happened with Flora and Herbert Bennet, and I ain't sayin' there has. They went together them three years, and, far as I can see, they think each other is better than in the beginnin'. Well, as I was sayin', it seemed to me that those two had ought to get married before long if they were ever goin' to, but I must confess I didn't see how they were any nearer it than when they started keepin' company."

"Herbert has been pretty handicapped," remarked Mrs. Cutting.

"Handicapped? Well, I rather guess he has! He was young when his father died, and when his mother had that dreadful sickness and had to go to the hospital, he couldn't keep up the taxes, and the interest on the mortgage got behindhand; the house was mortgaged when his father died, and it had to go; he's had to hire ever since. They're comin' here to live; you knew that, I s'pose?"

"Sophia, you don't mean his mother is coming here to live?"

"Why not? I'm mighty glad the poor woman's goin' to have a good home in her old age. She's a good woman as ever was, just as mild-spoken, and smart too. I'm tickled to death to think she's comin', and so's Flora. Flora sets her eyes by his mother."

"Well, you know your own business, but I must say I think it's a considerable undertaking."

"Well, I don't. I'd like to know what you'd have her do. Herbert can't afford to support two establishments, no more than he earns, and he ain't goin' to turn his mother out to earn her bread an' butter at her time of life, I rather guess. No; she's comin' here, and she's goin' to have the south chamber; she's goin' to furnish it. I never see a happier woman; and as for Herbert — well, he has had a hard time, and now things begin to look brighter; but I declare, about a year ago, as far as I could see, it didn't look as if he and Flora ever could get married. One evenin' the poor fellow came here, and he talked real plain; he said he felt as if he'd ought to. He said he'd been comin' here a long time, and he'd begun to think that he and Flora might keep on that way until they were gray, so far as he could help it. There he was, he said, workin' in Edgcomb's store at seven dollars a week, and had his mother to keep, and he couldn't see any prospect of anything better. He said maybe if he wasn't goin' with Flora she might get somebody else. 'It ain't fair to Flora,' said he. And with that he heaves a great sigh, and the first thing I knew, right before me, Flora she was in his lap, huggin' him, and cryin', and sayin' she'd never leave him for any man on the face of the earth, and she didn't ask anything any better than to wait. They'd both wait and be patient and trust in

God, and she was jest as happy as she could be, and she wouldn't change places with the Queen. First thing I knew I was cryin' too; I couldn't help it; and Herbert, poor fellow, he fetched a big sob himself, and I didn't think none the worse of him for it. 'Seems as if I must be sort of lackin' somehow, to make such a failure of things,' says he, kind of broken like.

"'You ain't lackin',' says Flora, real fierce like. 'It ain't you that's to blame. Fate's against you and always has been.'

"'Now you look round before you blame the Lord,' says I at that — for when folks say fate they always mean the Lord. 'Mebbe it ain't the Lord,' says I; 'mebbe it's folks. Wouldn't your uncle Hiram give you a lift, Herbert?'

"'Uncle Hiram!' says he; but not a bit scornful — real good-natured.

"'Why? I don't see why not,' says I. 'He always gives nice Christmas presents to you and your mother, don't he?'

"'Yes,' says he. 'He gives Christmas presents.'

"'Real nice ones?'

"'Yes,' said poor Herbert, kind of chucklin', but real good-natured. 'Last Christmas Uncle Hiram gave mother a silver card-case, and me a silver ash-receiver.'

"'But you don't smoke?' says I.

"'No,' says he, 'and mother hasn't got any visitin'-cards.'

"'I suppose he didn't know, along of not livin' in the same place,' says I.

"'No,' says he. 'They were real handsome things — solid; must have cost a lot of money.'

"'What would you do if you could get a little money, Herbert?' says I.

"Bless you! he knew quick enough. Didn't have to study over it a minute.

"'I'd buy that piece of land next your house here,' says he, 'and I'd keep cows and start a milk route. There's need of one here,' says he, 'and it's just what I've always thought I'd like to do; but it takes money,' he finishes up, with another of them heart-breakin' sighs of his, 'an' I ain't got a cent.'

"'Something will happen so you can have the milk route,' says Flora, and she kisses him right before me, and I was glad she did. I never approved of young folks bein' silly, but this was different. When a man feels as bad as Herbert Bennet did that day, if the woman that's goin' to marry him can comfort him any, she'd ought to.

"'Yes,' says I, 'something will surely happen. You jest keep your grit up, Herbert.'

"'How you women do stand by me!' says Herbert, and his voice broke again, and I was pretty near cryin'.

"'Well, we're goin' to stand by you jest as long as you are as good as you be now,' says I. 'The tide 'll turn before long.'

"I hadn't any more than got the words out of my mouth before the express drove up to the door, and there were three Christmas presents for Flora, early as it was, three days before Christmas. Christmas presents so long beforehand always make me a little suspicious, as if mebbe folks wanted other folks to be sure they were goin' to have something. Flora she'd always made real handsome presents to every one of them three that sent those that day. One was Herbert's aunt Harriet Morse, one was Cousin Jane Adkins over to Gorham, and the other was Mis' Crocker, she that was Emma Ladd; she's a second cousin of Flora's father's. Well, them three presents came, and we undid them. Then we looked at 'em. 'Great Jehosophat!' says I. Herbert he grinned, then he said something I didn't hear, and Flora she looked as if she didn't know whether to laugh or cry. There Flora she didn't have any money to put into presents, of course, but you know what beautiful fancy-work she does, and there she'd been workin' ever since the Christmas before, and she made a beautiful centre-piece and a bureau-scarf and a lace handkerchief for those three women, and there they had sent her a sort of a dewdab to wear in her hair! Pretty enough, looked as if it cost considerable — a pink rose with spangles, and a feather shootin' out of it; but Lord! if Flora had come out in that thing anywhere she'd go in Brookville, she'd scared the natives. It was all right where Herbert's aunt Harriet lived. Ayres is a city, but in this town, 'way from a railroad — goodness!

"Well, there was that; and Cousin Jane Adkins had sent her a Japanese silk shawl, all over embroidery, as handsome as a picture; but there was poor Flora wantin' some cotton cloth for her weddin' fix, and not a cent to buy a thing with. My sheets and pillow-cases and table-linen that I had from poor mother was about worn out, and Flora was wonderin' how she'd ever get any. But there Jane had sent that shawl, that cost nobody knew how much, when she knew Flora wanted the other things — because I'd told her. But Mis' Crocker's was the worst of all. She's a widow with a lot of money, and she's put on a good many airs. I dun'no' as you know her. No, I thought you didn't. Well, she does feel terrible airy. She sent poor Flora a set of chessmen, all red and white ivory, beautifully carved, and a table to keep 'em on. I must say I was so green I didn't know what they were when I first saw 'em.

Flora knew; she'd seen some somewhere she'd been.

"'For the land sake! what's them little dolls and horses for?' says I. 'It looks like Noah's ark without the ark.'

"'It's a set of chess and a table,' said Flora, and she looked ready to cry, poor child. She thought, when she got that great package, that she really had got something she wanted that time, sure.

"'Chess?' says I.

"'A game,' says Flora.

"'A game?' says I.

"'To play,' says she.

"'Do you know how to play it, Flora?' says I.

"'No,' says she.

"'Does Herbert?'

"'No.'

"'Well,' says I, and I spoke right out, 'of all the things to give anybody that needs things!'

"Flora was readin' the note that came with it. Jane Crocker said in the note that in givin' her Christmas present this year she was havin' a little eye on the future — and she underlined the future. She was twittin' Flora a little about her waitin' so long, and I knew it. Jane Crocker is a good woman enough, but she's got claws. She said she had an eye on the *underlined* future, and she said a chess set and a table were so stylish in a parlor. She didn't say a word about playin'.

"'Does she play that game?' says I to Flora.

"'I don't know,' says Flora. She didn't; I found out afterwards. She didn't know a single blessed thing about the game.

"Well, I looked at that present of poor Flora's, and I felt as if I should give up. 'How much do you s'pose that thing cost?' says I. Then I saw she had left the tag on. I looked. I didn't care a mite. I don't know where she got it. Wherever it was, she got cheated, if I know anything about it. There Jane Crocker had paid forty dollars for that thing.

"'Why didn't she give forty dollars for a Noah's ark and done with it?' says I. 'I'd jest as soon have one. Go and put it in the parlor,' says I.

"And poor Flora and Herbert lugged it into the parlor. She was almost cryin'.

"Well, the things kept comin' that Christmas. We both had a good many presents, and it did seem as if they were worse than they had ever been before. They had always been pretty bad. I don't care if I do say it."

There was a faint defiance in Sophia's voice. Mrs. Cutting and her daughters glanced imperceptibly at one another. A faint red showed on Mrs. Cutting's cheeks.

"Yes," repeated Sophia, firmly, "they always had been pretty bad. We had tried to be grateful, but it was the truth. There were so many things Flora and I wanted, and it did seem sometimes as if everybody that gave us Christmas presents sat up a week of Sundays tryin' to think of something to give us that we didn't want. There was Lizzie Starkwether; she gave us bed-shoes. She gave us bed-shoes the winter before, and the winter before that, but that didn't make a mite of difference. She kept right on givin' 'em, red-and-black bed-shoes. There she knits beautiful mittens and wristers, and we both wanted mittens or wristers; but no, we got bed-shoes. Flora and me never wear bed-shoes, and, what's more, I'd told Lizzie Starkwether so. I had a chance to do it when I thought I wouldn't hurt her feelin's. But that didn't make any difference; the bed-shoes come right along. I must say I was mad when I saw them that last time. 'I must say I don't call this a present; I call it a kick,' says I, and I'm ashamed to say I gave them bed-shoes a fling. There poor Flora had been sittin' up nights makin' a white apron trimmed with knit lace for Lizzie, because she knew she wanted one.

"Well, so it went; everything that come was a little more something we didn't want, especially Flora's; and she didn't say anything, but tried to look as if she was tickled to death; and she sent off the nice, pretty things she'd worked so hard to make, and every single one of them things, if I do say it, had been studied over an hour to every minute the ones she got had. Flora always tried not to give so much what she likes as what the one she's givin' to likes; and when I saw what she was gettin' back I got madder an' madder. I s'pose I wasn't showin' a Christian spirit, and Flora said so. She said she didn't give presents to get their worth back, and if they liked what she gave, that was worth more than anything. I could have felt that way if they'd been mine, but I couldn't when they were Flora's, and when the poor child had so little, and couldn't get married on account of it, too. Christmas mornin' came Herbert's rich uncle Hiram's present. It came while we were eatin' breakfast, about eight o'clock. We were rather late that mornin'. Well, the expressman drove into the yard, and he left a nice little package, and I saw the Leviston express mark on it, and I says to Flora, 'This must come from Herbert's uncle Hiram, and I shouldn't wonder if you had got something real nice.'

"Well, we undid it, and if there wasn't another silver card-case, the same style as Herbert's mother had given her the Christmas before. Well, Flora has got some visitin'-cards, but the idea of her carryin' a silver card-case like that when she went callin'! Why, she wouldn't have had anything else that come up to that card-case! Flora didn't say much, but I could see her lips quiver. She jest put it away, and pretty soon Herbert run in — he was out with the delivery-wagon from the store, and he stopped a second. He didn't stay long — he was too conscientious about his employer's time — but he stayed long enough to tell about his and his mother's Christmas presents from his uncle Hiram, and what do you think they had that time? Why, Herbert had a silver cigarette-case, and he never smokin' at all, and his mother had a cut-glass wine-set.

"Well, I didn't say much, but I was makin' up my mind. I was makin' it up slow, but I was makin' it up firm. Some more presents came that afternoon, and not a thing Flora wanted, except some ironin' holders from Cousin Ann Drake, and me a gingham apron from her. Yes, Flora did have another present she wanted, and that was a handkerchief come through the mail from the school-teacher that used to board here — a real nice, fine one. But the rest — well, there was a sofa-pillow painted with wild roses on boltin'-cloth, and there every sofa we'd got to lay down on in the house was this lounge here. We'd never had a sofa in the parlor, and Minerva Saunders — she sent it — knew it; and I'd like to know how much we could use a painted white boltin'-cloth pillow here? Minerva was rich, too, and I knew the pillow cost enough. And Mis' George Harris, she that was Minnie Beals — she was Flora's own cousin, you know — what did she send but a brass fire-set — poker and tongs and things — and here we ain't got an open fire-place in the house, and she knew it. But Minnie never did have much sense; I never laid it up against her. She meant well, and she's sent Flora some beautiful napkins and table-cloths; I told her that was what she wanted for a weddin'-present. Well, as I was sayin', I was makin' up my mind slow but firm, and by afternoon it was made up. Says I to Flora: 'I wish you'd go over to Mr. Martin's and ask him if I can have his horse and sleigh this afternoon. Tell him I'll pay him.' He never takes any pay, but I always offer. Flora said: 'Why, Aunt Sophia, you ain't goin' out this afternoon! It looks as if it would snow every minute.'

"'Yes, I be,' says I.

"Well, Flora went over and asked, and Mr. Martin said I was welcome to the horse and sleigh — he's always real accommodatin' — and he hitched up himself and brought it over about one o'clock. I thought I'd start early, because it did threaten snow. I got Flora out of the way — sent her down to the store to get some sugar; we were goin' to make cake when I got home, and we were all out of powdered sugar. When that sleigh come I jest bundled all them presents — except the apron and holders and the two or three other things that was presents, because the folks that give 'em had studied up what Flora wanted, and give to her instead of themselves — an' I stowed them all in that sleigh, under the seat and on it, and covered them up with the robe.

"Then I wrapped up real warm, because it was bitter cold — seemed almost too cold to snow — and I put a hot soapstone in the sleigh, and I gathered up the reins, an' I slapped 'em over the old horse's back, and I set out.

"I thought I'd go to Jane Crocker's first — I wanted to get rid of that chess-table; it took up so much room in the sleigh I hadn't any place to put my feet, and the robe kept slippin' off it. So I drove right there. Jane was to home; the girl came to the door, and I went into the parlor. I hadn't been to call on Jane for some time, and she'd got a number of new things I hadn't seen, and the first thing I saw was a chess-table and all them little red and white Noah's-ark things, jest like the one she sent us. When Jane come in, dressed in black silk stiff enough to stand alone — though she wa'n't goin' anywheres and it looked like snow — I jest stood right up. I'd brought in the table and the box of little jiggers, and I goes right to the point. I had to. I had to drive six miles to Ayres before I got through, and there it was spittin' snow already.

"'Good-afternoon, Jane,' says I. 'I've brought back your presents.'

"Jane she kind of gasped, and she turned pale. She has a good deal of color; she's a pretty woman; well, it jest slumped right out of her cheeks. 'Mercy! Sophia,' says she, 'what do you mean?'

"'Jest what I say, Jane,' says I. 'You've sent Flora some playthings that cost forty dollars — you left the tags on, so we know — and they ain't anything she has any use for. She don't know how to play chess, and neither does Herbert; and if they did know, they wouldn't neither of 'em have any time, unless it was Sundays, and then it would be wicked.'

"'Oh, Lord! Sophia,' says she, kind of chokin', 'I don't know how to play myself, but I've got one for an ornament, and I thought Flora —'

"'Flora will have to do without forty-dollar ornaments, if ever she gets money enough to get married at all,' says I, 'and I don't think a Noah's ark set on a table marked up in squares is much of an ornament, anyhow.'

"I didn't say any more. I jest marched out and left the presents. But Jane she came runnin' after me. 'Sophia,' says she — and she spoke as if she was sort of scared. She never had much spunk, for all she looks so up an' comin' — 'Sophia,' says she, 'I thought she'd like it. I thought — '

"'No, you didn't, Jane Crocker,' says I. 'You jest thought what you'd like to give, and not what she'd like to have.'

"'What would she like to have?' says she, and she was 'most cryin'. 'I'll get her anything she wants, if you'll jest tell me, Sophia.'

"'I ain't goin' to tell you, Jane,' says I, but I spoke softer, for I saw that she meant well, after all — 'I ain't goin' to tell you. You jest put yourself in her place; you make believe you was a poor young girl goin' to get married, and you think over what little the poor child has got now and what she has to set alongside *new* things, and you kind of study it out for yourself,' says I. And then I jest said good-by, though she kept callin' after me, and I run out and climbed in the sleigh and tucked myself in and drove off.

"The very next day Jane Crocker sent Flora a beautiful new carpet for the front chamber, and a rug to go with it. She knew Flora was goin' to have the front chamber fixed up when she got married; she'd heard me say so; and the carpet was all worn out.

"Well, I kept right on. I carried back Cousin Abby Adkins's white silk shawl, and she acted awful mad; but she thought better of it as I was goin' out to the sleigh, and she called after me to know what Flora wanted, and I told her jest what I had Jane Crocker. And I carried back Minerva Saunders's boltin'-cloth sofa-pillow, and she was more astonished than anything else — she was real good-natured. You know how easy she is. She jest laughed after she'd got over bein' astonished. 'Why,' says she, 'I don't know but it *is* kind of silly, now I come to think of it. I declare I clean forgot you didn't have a sofa in the parlor. When I've been in there I've been so took up seein' you and Flora, Sophia, that I never took any account at all of the furniture.'

"So I went away from there feelin' real good, and the next day but one there come a nice hair-cloth sofa for Flora to put in the parlor.

"Then I took back Minnie Harris's fire-set, and she acted kind of dazed. 'Why, don't you think it's handsome?' says she. You know she's a young thing, younger than Flora. She's always called me Aunt Sophia, too. 'Why, Aunt Sophia,' says she, 'didn't Flora think it was handsome?'

"'Handsome enough, child,' says I, and I couldn't help laughin' myself, she looked like sech a baby — 'handsome enough, but what did you think Flora was goin' to do with a poker and tongs to poke a fire, when there ain't any fire to poke?'

"Then Minnie she sort of giggled. 'Why, sure enough, Aunt Sophia,' says she. 'I never thought of that.'

"'Where did you think she would put them?' says I. 'On the parlor mantel-shelf for ornaments?'

"Then Minnie she laughed sort of hysterical. 'Give 'em right here, Aunt Sophia,' says she.

"The next day she sent a clock — that wasn't much account, though it was real pretty; it won't go long at a time — but it looks nice on the parlor shelf, and it was so much better than the poker and tongs that I didn't say anything. It takes sense to give a present, and Minnie Harris never had a mite, though she's a pretty little thing.

"Then I took home Lizzie Starkwether's bed-shoes, and she took it the worst of all.

"'Don't they fit?' says she.

"'Fit well 'nough,' says I. 'We don't want 'em.'

"'I'd like to know why not,' says she.

"'Because you've given us a pair every Christmas for three years,' says I, 'and I've told you we never wear bed-shoes; and even if we did wear 'em,' says I, 'we couldn't have worn out the others to save our lives. When we go to bed, we go to sleep,' says I. 'We don't travel round to wear out shoes. We've got two pairs apiece laid away,' says I, 'and I think you'd better give these to somebody that wants 'em — mebbe somebody that you've been givin' mittens to for three years, that don't wear mittens.'

"Well, she was hoppin', but she got over it, too; and I guess she did some thinkin', for in a week came the prettiest mittens for each of us I ever laid eyes on, and Minerva herself came over and called, and thanked Flora for her apron as sweet as pie.

"Well, I went to all the others in town, and then I started for Ayres, and carried back the dewdab to Herbert's aunt Harriet Morse. I hated to do that, for I didn't know her very well; but I went, and she was real nice. She made me drink a cup of tea and eat a slice of her cake, and she thanked me for comin'. She said she didn't know what young girls liked, and she had an idea that they cared more about something to dress up in than anything else, even if they didn't have a great deal to do with, and she had ought to have known better than to send such a silly thing. She spoke real kind about Herbert, and hoped he could get married before long; and the next day she sent Flora a pair of beautiful blankets, and now she's given Flora all her bed linen and towels for a weddin'-

present. I heated up my soapstone in her kitchen oven and started for home. It was almost dark, and snowin' quite hard, and she said she hated to have me go, but I said I didn't mind. I was goin' to stop at Herbert's uncle Hiram's on my way home. You know he lives in Leviston, half-way from Ayres.

"When I got there it was snowin' hard, comin' real thick.

"I drew up at the front gate and hitched the horse, and waded through the snow to the front door and rung the bell; and Uncle Hiram's housekeeper came to the door. She is a sort of cousin of his — a widow woman from Ayres. I don't know as you know who she is. She's a dreadful lackada'sical woman, kind of pretty, long-faced and slopin'-shouldered, and she speaks kind of slow and sweet. I asked if Mr. Hiram Snell was in, and she said she guessed so, and asked me in, and showed me into the sittin'-room, which was furnished rich; but it was awful dirty and needed dustin'. I guess she ain't much of a housekeeper. Uncle Hiram was in the sittin'-room, smokin' a pipe and readin'. You know Hiram Snell. He's kind of gruff-spoken, but he ain't bad-meanin'. It's more because he's kind of blunderin' about little things, like most men; ain't got a small enough grip to fit 'em. Well, he stood up when I come in. He knew me by sight, and I said who I was — that I was aunt to Flora Bell that his nephew Herbert Bennet was goin' to marry; and he asked me to sit down, but I said I couldn't because I had to drive a matter of three miles to get home, and it was snowin' so hard. Then I out with that little fool card-case, and I said I'd brought it back.

"'What's the matter? Ain't it good enough?' says he, real short. He's got real shaggy eyebrows, an' I tell you his eyes looked fierce under 'em.

"'Too good,' says I. 'Flora she ain't got anything good enough to go with it. This card-case can't be carried by a woman unless she has a handsome silk dress, and fine white kid gloves, and a sealskin sacque, and a hat with an ostrich feather,' says I.

"'Do you want me to give her all those things to go with the card-case?' says he, kind of sarcastic.

"'If you did, they'd come back quicker than you could say Jack Robinson,' says I, for I was gettin' mad myself.

"But all of a sudden he burst right out laughin'. 'Well,' says he, 'you've got horse-sense, an' that's more than I can say of most women.' Then he takes the card-case and he looks hard at it. 'Why, Mrs. Pendergrass said she'd be sure to like it!' says he. 'Said she'd got one for Herbert's mother last year. Mrs. Pendergrass buys all my Christmas presents for me. I don't make many.'

"'I shouldn't think you'd better if you can't get more sensible ones to send,' says I. I knew I was saucy, but he was kind of smilin', and I laughed when I said it, though I meant it all the same.

"'Why, weren't Herbert's all right?' says he.

"'Right?' says I. 'Do you know what he had last year?'

"'No, I don't,' says he.

"'Well, last year you sent him a silver ash-tray, and his mother a card-case, and this year he had a silver cigarette-case, and his mother a cut-glass wine-set.'

"'Well?'

"'Nothin', only Herbert never smokes, and his mother hasn't got any visitin'-cards, and she don't have much wine, I guess.'

"Hiram Snell laughed again. 'Well, I left it all to Mrs. Pendergrass,' says he. 'I never thought she had brains to spare, but then I never thought it took brains to buy Christmas presents.'

"'It does,' says I, — 'brains and consider'ble love for the folks you are buyin' for.'

"'Christmas is tomfoolery, anyhow,' says he.

"'That's as you look at it,' says I.

"He stood eyin' me sort of gruff, and yet as if he were sort of tickled at the same time. 'Well,' says he, finally, 'you've brought this fool thing back. Now what shall I give your niece instead?'

"'I don't go round beggin' for presents,' says I.

"'How the devil am I going to get anything that she'll like any better if I don't know?' says he. 'And Mrs. Pendergrass can't help me out any. You've got to say something.'

"'I sha'n't,' says I, real set. 'You ain't no call to give my niece anything, anyway; you ain't no call to give her anything she wants, and you certainly ain't no call to give her anything she don't want.'

"'You don't believe in keepin' presents you don't want?'

"'No,' says I, 'I don't — and thankin' folks for 'em as if you liked 'em. It's hypocrisy.'

"He kind of grunted, and laughed again.

"'It don't make any odds about Flora,' says I; 'and as for your nephew and your sister, you know about them and what they want as well as I do, or you'd ought to. I ain't goin' to tell you.'

"'So Maria hasn't got any cards, and Herbert don't smoke,' says he, and he grinned as if it was awful funny.

"Well, I thought it was time for me to be goin', and jest then Mrs. Pendergrass came in with a lighted lamp. It had darkened all of a sudden, and I could hear the sleet on the window, and there I had three miles to drive.

"So I started, and Hiram Snell he followed me to the door. He seemed sort of anxious about my goin' out in the storm, and come out himself through all the snow, and unhitched my horse and held him till I got nicely tucked in the sleigh. Then jest as I gathered up the reins, he says, speakin' up loud against the wind,

"'When is Herbert and your niece goin' to get married?'

"'When Herbert gets enough money to buy a piece of land and some stock and start a milk route,' says I. Then off I goes."

Sophia paused for a climax. Her guests were listening, breathless.

"Well, what did he give Herbert?" asked Mrs. Cutting.

"He gave him three thousand dollars to buy that land and some cows and put up a barn," said Sophia, and her audience drew a long, simultaneous breath.

"That was great," said Eunice.

"And he's made Flora a wedding-present of five shares in the Ayres street-railroad stock, so she should have a little spendin'-money," said Sophia.

"I call him a pretty generous man," said Abby Dodd.

"Generous enough," said Sophia Lane, "only he didn't know how to steer his generosity."

The guests rose; they were looking somewhat uncomfortable and embarrassed. Sophia went into the bedroom to get their wraps, letting a breath of ice into the sitting-room. While she was gone the guests conferred hastily with one another.

When she returned, Mrs. Cutting faced her, not unamiably, but confusedly. "Now look here, Sophia Lane," said she, "I want you to speak right out. You needn't hesitate. We all want the truth. Is — anything the matter with our presents we brought to-day?"

"Use your own jedgment," replied Sophia Lane.

"Where are those presents we brought?" asked Mrs. Cutting. She and her daughters all looked sober and doubtful, but not precisely angry.

"They are in the parlor," replied Sophia.

"Suppose you get them," said Mrs. Cutting.

When Sophia returned with the alcohol-lamp and afternoon-tea kettle, the finger-bowls and the doilies, the guests had on their wraps. Abby Dodd and Eunice at once went about tying up the presents. Mrs. Cutting looked on. Sophia got her little shawl and hood. She was going out to the barn to assist her guests in getting their horse out.

"Has Flora got any dishes?" asked Mrs. Cutting, thoughtfully.

"No, she hasn't got anything but her mother's china tea-set," replied Sophia. "She hasn't got any good dishes for common use."

"No dinner-set?"

"No; mine are about used up, and I've been careful with 'em too."

Mrs. Cutting considered a minute longer. "Has she got some good tumblers?" she asked.

"No, she hasn't. We haven't any too many tumblers in the house."

"How is she off for napkins?" asked Eunice, tying up her doilies.

"She ain't any too well off. She's had a dozen give her, and that's all."

The guests, laden with the slighted wedding-gifts, followed Sophia through the house, the kitchen, and the clean, cold woodshed to the barn. Sophia slid back the heavy doors.

"Well, good-by, Sophia," said Mrs. Cutting. "We've had a nice time, and we've enjoyed seeing Flora's presents."

"Yes, so have I," said Eunice.

"I think she's fared real well," said Abby.

"Yes, she has," said Sophia.

"We shall be over in good season," said Eunice.

"Yes, we shall," assented Abby.

Sophia untied the horse, which had been fastened to a ring beside the door; still the guests did not move to get into the sleigh. A curious air of constraint was over them. Sophia also looked constrained and troubled. Her poor faithful face peering from the folds of her gray wool hood was defiant and firm, but still anxious. She looked at Mrs. Cutting, and the two women's eyes met; there was a certain wistfulness in Sophia's.

"I think a good deal of Flora," said she, and there was a hint of apology in her tone.

Simultaneously the three women moved upon Sophia, their faces cleared; lovely expressions of sympathy and kindly understanding appeared upon them.

"Good-by, Sophia," said Mrs. Cutting, and kissed her.

"Good-by, Cousin Sophia," said the daughters, and they also kissed her.

When they drove out of the snowy yard, three smiling faces turned back for a last greeting to Sophia. She slid together the heavy barn doors. She was smiling happily, though there were tears in her eyes.

"Everybody in this world means to be pretty good to other folks," she muttered to herself, "and when they ain't, it ain't always their fault; sometimes it's other folks'."

LUCY

Old Lysander Avery passed out of Ebbit's store with his arms full of parcels, when Ebbit himself started and called after him: "Hullo! Hold on a minute, Lysander; there's a letter for you in the post-office."

Old Lysander turned slowly.

Ebbit came up with the letter, eying it himself as he advanced. "It's a letter from your daughter, I guess," he said; "I 'most forgot it."

"It ain't the day for the letter," remarked old Lysander, anxiously. He took the letter and examined the superscription. "Hope she ain't sick, nor nothin'," he muttered.

"It's her handwriting," said the storekeeper, encouragingly.

"Yes, 'tis," said old Lysander, and put the letter carefully in his pocket.

The storekeeper and his gossips stood back, while old Lysander passed out.

"S'pose he's been buyin' all that truck for his little grand-child."

The storekeeper nodded. "Sets his eyes by her," he said; "thinks she's just about perfection."

Old Lysander plodded homeward. The snow was deep, and trodden as hard as a floor. The weather was very clear and freezing. Lysander's garments were old but warm, and his blood was still reasonably quick. He clasped numerous parcels to his sides; others dangled by their strings from his fingers.

It was quite a pretentious old farm-house which Lysander Avery owned, and which his grandfather and father had owned before him. It was the struggle of Lysander's life to keep this place in perfect repair on his tiny income. He eyed it with pride and affection as he drew near.

He went around to the door upon the south side. He saw a toss of yellow past the kitchen window, then the door flew open and little Lucy stood there, her blue frock fluttering and her yellow fleece floating, and her two little hands waving with welcome.

Little Lucy did not say one word, but she looked at her grand-father coming with his bundles, and her face seemed to deepen with joy rather than smile. Not a muscle of her little, serious mouth seemed to move, but she was radiant all at once. Old Lysander regarded her with adoration. "Well, ducky darlin', there you be," said he. "Guess you'd better stand back and let grandpa in; it's dreadful cold."

A woman's voice echoed his: "Yes, stan' back and let your grandpa in; you're coldin' the house all off," said the voice, which was admonitory, but not coercive.

Old Lysander carefully unloaded his packages on the kitchen table, his wife assisting. Little Lucy stood delicately aloof, rising slightly on the tips of her toes, bending forward with the air of timid curiosity of a bird. Lysander looked at her, then he nudged his wife, and she looked.

"What you watchin' out so sharp for, ducky darlin'?" asked old Lysander. Little Lucy bent her head and turned her face to one side, until only the curve of one baby cheek was visible; then she laughed, very softly, as if to herself. "I s'pose she thinks grandpa has got somethin' in them bundles for her Christmas," said the old man, with infinite enjoyment of the situation.

"Mebbe she does," said his wife, rapturously.

"And I don't see why she should, nuther," said Lysander.

His wife laughed, her mouth widening in a curve of inane innocence, like a baby's. Sylvia Avery was small and exceedingly thin, with the sort of thinness which suggests old china. Little Lucy resembled her. They moved and spoke alike; both voices had a trick of always dropping at the last syllable.

"You'd better set down in your little chair by the stove and keep warm, ducky darlin'," said old Lysander.

"Yes, you sit down, Lucy, and mebbe you can finish your dolly's apron before supper," said Sylvia.

Little Lucy obeyed. She seated herself in the tiny rocking-chair. It was in a warm corner near the cooking-stove, where the waning light from a western window fell. There was a clear, golden sunset, with rose and violet at the horizon-line, visible beyond her.

The old man and woman looked at her, then at each other, with a rapture of acquiescence over their common idol; then they went with the packages into the icy sitting-room across the hall.

In the sitting-room they began stowing away the parcels in a chimney closet, when suddenly old Lysander started. "I declare I forgot all about it, with all this to-do about Christmas," he said. "I've got a letter from Emma. Ebbit ran after me with it when I was goin' out of the store."

Sylvia turned pale. "It ain't the day for the letter. Oh, Lysander, you don't suppose she's sick, do you?"

"It's her writin'," said Lysander.

Sylvia opened the letter, and began to read eagerly. "She ain't comin'," she quavered.

"I was afeard so when I saw the letter."

"Yes; the woman they expected to take her place, the one that worked there so long before she was married, is sick. They won't let Emma off. She can't come."

Old Lysander's face was gloomy. He stood looking at his wife.

"That ain't all," she said, faintly. "She — wants little Lucy —"

"Wants little Lucy?"

"She wants — little Lucy to come to-morrow, and spend Christmas with her. She's dreadful disappointed, she's been lottin' so on comin' home; she says it's makin' her about sick, an' she says she thinks we might let her have little Lucy. She says Lucy can go to the store with her some. Then she says she'll have one evenin' that she can take her to the theatre to see 'Cinderella,' and a woman that boards to the same place wants to take her to an afternoon performance to see 'Jack and the Bean-stalk,' and the other boarders want to get up a little Christmas-tree for her. She says she can see all the stores trimmed up for Christmas, and she'll have a better time than she ever had in her whole life."

Old Lysander Avery looked at his wife. "We've been lottin' a good deal on havin' of her here Christmas," he said.

"Yes, we have," said Sylvia. Her mild blue eyes looked suddenly pink around the lids.

They continued to look at each other. Sylvia shivered perceptibly. "You're ketchin' your death of cold, mother," said Lysander, with sudden tenderness.

"I s'pose we've got to make up our minds quick, if — she's goin' to-morrow," chattered Sylvia.

"Yes, I s'pose so."

"I s'pose she'd have — a beautiful time; it would be somethin' for her to remember all her life," she said, with little nervous gasps for breath.

"Yes, I s'pose so," said Lysander.

"And I do s'pose it would be a sight of comfort to poor Emma."

"Mebbe it would."

Then the two, hand-in-hand, passed out of the cold room, across the little entry to the warm kitchen, where little Lucy sat. Old Lysander approached little Lucy and stood over her.

"Well, grandpa has got somethin' real nice to tell little Lucy," said he. She looked up inquiringly at him, while Sylvia shut the oven door and lighted a lamp. "It's somethin' real nice," he went on, in a voice of unfaltering cheerfulness. "Lucy's aunt Emma that she 'ain't ever seen, because she's only been living with grandpa and grandma six months, and Aunt Emma 'ain't been home, wants her to come and stay with her in the big city where she lives. Aunt Emma was comin' here to spend Christmas, but they can't spare her from the store where she works at the glove-counter, 'cause the lady that was goin' to take her place is sick, and she feels real bad, and she wants little Lucy to come and see her. Mother, you'd better tell her what her aunt Emma says."

Sylvia went over the list of promised joys in a quavering voice, with faithful, wistful eyes fixed on the child's changing face. "you want to go, don't you, Lucy?" she asked, after she had finished the list.

"You and grandpa goin' too?" inquired little Lucy.

Old Lysander looked at Sylvia. "No, ducky darlin'," he said.

"I don't want to go unless you an' grandma are goin' too," Lucy said.

The old people exchanged glances of rapture.

"Grandpa an' grandma are too old to go traipsin' round the country in sech dreadful cold weather," said Lysander. "They can keep real nice and quiet here, and have a real nice Christmas, thinkin' how little Lucy an' Aunt Emma are enjoyin' themselves."

"An' you'll love Aunt Emma jest as well as you love us, when you come to see her," said Sylvia. It ended in little Lucy, with her inborn docility, acceding to the plan for her visit. Early the next morning they started for the railway station.

Old Lysander dragged little Lucy to the station on a sled. Sylvia kissed her goodbye, then she went in and shut the door hurriedly. Little Lucy was so well wrapped against the cold that she looked like a shapeless bundle of love and woe as she sat on the sled. She swallowed hard to keep the sobs back as she slid along over the creaking snow behind her grandfather, and stared through tears at the early winter morning. It was clear and very cold, and the smoke arose from the chimneys in straight columns of rose-flushed blue.

When they reached the railroad station the train was already coming in. Old Lysander hurried little Lucy onto the train. "Goodbye," he said, in a husky voice. "Mind you don't lose your ticket, and don't you get off till you get there." Then he rubbed his rough cheek hard against her little soft one, and little Lucy was in the train going to Boston. Old Lysander stood on the platform watching the train as it rolled out of the station. "She got a seat by the winder," he told Sylvia when he got home.

Little Lucy, travelling to Boston, sat close to the window and gazed out earnestly. In spite of herself the sight of the swiftly moving, unfamiliar landscape amused her, and diverted her mind from the terror of the strange new world into which she was plunging, a little tender girl all alone by herself. When the conductor took her ticket he gave her a friendly little pat on the shoulder, and said, "Going on a journey, sis?" and no one else spoke to her. She ate her luncheon by-and-by, and continued looking out of the window. Presently it began to snow, then it snowed steadily all the rest of the way. It grew dusky early in the afternoon. Little Lucy nestled into her corner and watched gravely the rapid recedence of the telegraph-poles and shadowy trees and houses through the driving veil of the snow. At last the train entered the great station in Boston, and everybody gathered up their belongings and arose, and then little Lucy became conscious of a roaring in her ears, and her heart seemed to shake her with its beating. She rose, clutching her little bag very tightly. Her knees trembled, her forehead puckered, she felt a sob in her throat. She followed the other passengers out of the car and off the train. The red-faced conductor jumped her down the high steps.

"Here we are, sis," he said. "Anybody expecting you?"

"My aunt Emma," replied Lucy, chokingly.

"All right," said the red-faced conductor. "Guess you'll find her in the waiting-room right ahead."

But Lucy, trotting along in the wake of the other passengers with nervous haste, did not reach the waiting-room.

Suddenly from a group of waiting people drawn up at the side of the platform sprang a beautiful and rather young lady.

"Here she is, here she is, Agnes," she exclaimed, in a very soft voice, and she came straight with a sort of gentle rush at little Lucy. She stood looking down at her, smiling out of her fluff of fur and wave of plumes, then outstretched her soft, velvet arms, and little Lucy was clasped close, and was dimly conscious in the midst of her surprise and joy of the scent of violets, and the singing of silken skirts, and the soft tickle of fur against her cheeks. Then the lady bent down and kissed her with a delicate caress. "Dear little Lucy, I knew you the minute I saw you," she murmured; "little darling. So you've come to see your auntie, haven't you, all alone such a long distance? Are you tired, darling? Of course you're tired. We'll go straight home, and you shall have your supper and go to bed. Agnes dear, it is little Lucy. You are little Lucy, aren't you, dear?"

"Yes, ma'am," replied Lucy, her voice muffled against the soft velvet and lace and fur at the lady's neck.

"Of course you are. I knew you the minute I saw you. You are just like your dear mamma. Agnes, isn't she a darling?"

Then another young lady, very much like the first, only she was taller and younger, and not quite so pretty, welcomed little Lucy, and also kissed and embraced her; and then a man in a sort of uniform, which made Lucy think of him as a soldier and wonder where his gun was, came in response to a gesture from the first lady, and Lucy was instructed to give him her check, and then she was swept away by the two ladies, who seemed to hover around her and envelop her, into a beautiful dark-blue carriage with little pictures on the doors. Then she sat beside the first lady on a very soft cushion, and the other lady sat opposite, and both beamed at her.

"Dear little thing," said the lady called Agnes. "Isn't she a dear, sister?"

"I *think* she's a dear," responded the other lady, with enthusiasm, and she put her arm around little Lucy as they sat in the carriage and drew her lovingly into the soft nest of velvet and fur which smelled of violets. "How are they all — grandmother and grandfather?" said she.

"Yes, how did you leave them, sweetheart?" asked Agnes.

"They are very well, I thank you," replied little Lucy, shyly; and that question soothed a certain wonder which had come over her to hear her aunt Emma called sister by the lady named Agnes. She knew Aunt Emma's only sister had been her own mother.

"You dear, quaint little thing!" said the lady who had been called sister. "Hasn't she a dear, precise little way of speaking, just like her grandmother Agnes?"

"Hasn't she?" responded Agnes, admiringly.

"I don't know what John will say to her," said sister. "I expect she will make him forget his aches and pains. Do you want to see Uncle John, darling?"

Little Lucy regarded her with intense bewilderment.

"Why, don't you want to see Uncle John?" repeated sister; and Lucy hurriedly replied,

"Yes, ma'am"; but she was still dazed.

Then came another question which puzzled her still more. "How is your dear papa, sweetheart?" asked Agnes.

Little Lucy turned pale, and stared at her.

"How is your dear papa? Didn't he feel pretty badly to have his little girl go away without him?" asked sister.

Little Lucy looked at her with a shocked, grieved, reproachful stare.

"Why don't you answer, darling?" sister said, with her face close to Lucy's.

"Papa is — dead!" Lucy burst out, with a great sob of excitement and sorrow. "Papa is dead!"

Sister gave a start, then she held her off and looked at her, and then she and Agnes looked at each other, and both of them were very white.

"Sister, what does she mean?" gasped Agnes.

"I don't know," gasped sister. "Darling," she said, very gently, to Lucy, "I asked you how your dear papa was. You mistook. You did not mean to say that —"

"My papa is dead," repeated little Lucy, with painful and reproachful firmness.

The ladies looked at each other.

"Sister, it is impossible," said Agnes — "impossible. We had the telegram when she started, and certainly nothing had happened then. Dear, your papa was quite well when you left him, was he not?"

"My papa is dead," repeated little Lucy, and then she began to cry.

Sister immediately fondled her and soothed her. "There, there, you darling! you shall not be troubled any more about it," she said. "You are all tired out with your journey, and you don't know what you are talking about. Agnes, speak to Thomas to drive a little faster. We will go straight home, and you shall have some nice dinner, and go to bed and get rested. Poor little soul, it was cruel to send her such a long journey alone."

It was half an hour before the carriage stopped before some tall stone steps of a tall house. Another soldier opened the carriage door, helped sister and Agnes to get out, then lifted out little Lucy and carried her up the steps as if she were a baby. The soldier carried her into a warm, beautiful hall like a room, with a great fireplace full of blazing logs, and a carved stair rising out of it. Up this carved stair little Lucy was carried into the loveliest little room, which seemed to fairly float out to meet her, with draperies of lace and pink silk at the windows and on the bed. The carpet was all strewn with roses, and there was a little couch with a quantity of pillows all roses, and there were little china trays all sprinkled with roses on the dresser. Little Lucy was carried over to the couch in front of the fire blazing on a little, white-tiled hearth, and a pretty girl with a tiny white cap and white apron, whom sister and Agnes called Louise, took off her little coat and red hat, and her mittens and rubbers and leggings. Then her feet were lifted, and she was bidden to lie down and rest.

Then sister came and sat down beside her and kissed her and held her little hands. "Auntie's little darling," she said, and little Lucy felt that she loved her very much. She smiled timidly, and her little fingers clung to sister's. "You blessed little soul," cried sister; "she did get all tired out with her journey, didn't she? No, don't try to talk, darling. Just lie still and get rested."

Then Louise brought a cup of chocolate and a most delicious little cake on a lovely plate, and while she sipped and ate she became aware of a tall, brown-bearded gentleman with a stick, upon which he leaned quite heavily, regarding her from the doorway. "Here she is, John," said sister. "Here is Uncle John, darling."

The tall gentleman advanced and spoke very kindly to Lucy. "Well, little one," said he, "had a pretty hard journey all alone, did you not?" Then before Lucy could say anything he turned to sister.

"I've said all along it was cruelty to children to send her here all alone," he said. "Frank ought to be ashamed of himself. He isn't fit to take care of a child. Never will be anything but a boy himself. She never would have come alone if I had not been laid up with this confounded rheumatism, I can tell you that much. Of course she is about used up with it. Doesn't take half an eye to see that. I've telephoned Frank. He's all right. I told him that Lucy had arrived in a very alarming condition, and we had sent for the doctor at once; that she was out of her —" But sister, and Agnes, who had just entered, stopped him.

"Don't, don't, I beg of you, John," cried sister, with an alarmed glance at Lucy, and Agnes echoed her. "John," she said, with a warning touch on his shoulder, "you forget that the child can hear."

John desisted with a sort of growl. "Well," he said, "Dr. Jerrold is coming. They telephoned that he was in and would be here right away. I think that child had better go to bed."

"Perhaps she had, John," agreed sister. "I will have her put to bed."

"And give her some gruel and beefsteak," said Uncle John, as he went out of the room.

At last the doctor came. "I suppose your papa is pretty lonesome without you," he said, with a view to professional facetiousness, and the child made her reply as before, with a piteous reiteration.

"We have just telephoned, and he is quite well," whispered

Agnes.

"All right, little one," said the doctor, hastily, and directly, with a bewildering inconsequence, inquired of little Lucy if she liked dolls.

"It is a very perplexing case," he owned to sister and Agnes and Uncle John outside the room. "She seems to be in a perfectly normal condition. Her pulse is a little quick, and there are slight symptoms of cerebral excitement, but very slight, and easily accounted for. She is very young, and a very nervous child to travel alone."

"What shall we do when she says her papa is dead?" inquired Agnes, almost weeping.

"Don't contradict her on any account," said the doctor, impressively — "not on any account." The doctor was a handsome, fair, keen young man, with a very impressive, nervous manner. "Not on any account," he repeated; "and if she should make other statements which you have reason to know are erroneous, let her have her way. Don't contradict her in the slightest degree."

"She will be all right to-morrow, I dare say," said Uncle John, when the doctor had gone; "but all the same, Frank ought to be ashamed of himself, and I mean to tell him so, sending that little thing all that way alone."

"Isn't she a dear little thing?" said Agnes, effusively.

"Dear enough," replied Uncle John; "and dear or not, a child ought to be treated like a child, and not like a grown-up woman sufragist, coming all that distance alone."

Sister sighed. "There is another topic on which the dear child is not quite herself," she said. "She said, when I alluded to Cleveland, that she had not come from Cleveland, but from Brookfield, Massachusetts, and had started this morning."

"I hope you did not contradict her, sister," said Agnes, anxiously.

"No; I immediately changed the subject, and talked about taking her to see 'Cinderella,' and she seemed delighted."

"She will be all right in the morning," said Uncle John.

But poor little Lucy was not all right in the morning. She had her breakfast in bed, much to her amazement, as that was something which she had never done. There was another thing which puzzled Lucy beyond anything. She could see by the little clock on her mantel-shelf that it was nine o'clock, and why was not Aunt Emma at the store, at her glove-counter? Why was she remaining at home so late in the morning, when she had not been able to leave to go home to Brookfield? Lucy supposed that Agnes must work at the glove-counter with Aunt Emma, and she also was still at home. Finally little Lucy, having suddenly decided that Aunt Emma was staying home on her account, because she seemed to think that she was sick, timidly said something about it.

It was almost the first question that she had volunteered. "Aunt Emma," she said, in a little, trembling voice.

"Did you speak, sweetheart?" asked sister, looking at her in a bewildered way, with a glance of alarm at Agnes.

"Yes, Aunt Emma," said Lucy, and both of the ladies turned pale; but sister spoke up quite bravely and collectedly.

"Yes, dear; what is it?" she asked.

"I wondered," said little Lucy, "why you did not go to the store, when it is so late."

"The store?" said sister, vaguely.

"The store?" echoed Agnes.

"Lucy looked at her. "The store where you sell gloves," said she, comprehensively.

The two ladies gasped. But sister did not lose her self-command.

"We are going very soon, darling," said she, "very soon; don't worry."

"I ain't sick," said little Lucy.

"No, of course you are not, sweetheart," said Agnes, hastily.

"Very soon we will all go to the store and see the pretty Christmas things," said sister.

But very soon the two ladies went out of the room and clutched each other in the hall.

"Louise! Louise!" cried sister, and Louise came hurrying out of her room. "Telephone immediately and bid Dr. Jerrold hurry up here at once," said sister, faintly. Then she whispered to Agnes, when Louise had slipped hastily away, "She is terribly out of her head this morning."

"Yes, she is," assented Agnes.

"The store and the glove-counter!" gasped sister.

"But it was wonderful how you kept your presence of mind and did not contradict her," said Agnes, admiringly.

"I am going to have Dr. Jerrold send us a trained nurse," said sister. "I don't feel competent to deal with such a dangerous case. And Frank must be telegraphed at once."

"I think I had better see John and have that done without any delay," said Agnes.

However, when the doctor arrived, he said in his opinion

Lucy was better, and it was not necessary to have the nurse; but the telegram was already sent.

"Let him come," growled Uncle John, whose rheumatism was worse. "It will do him good to worry all the way here; teach him a lesson, and he can spend Christmas with Lucy."

"She will enjoy seeing the shop-windows," said Agnes. "She quite brightened up when I spoke of that."

It was still snowing, but that made no difference. Little Lucy went with sister and Agnes in a covered sleigh, and the city streets in the shopping district were cleared away enough to enable them to drive about without much trouble.

"It is very fortunate that little Lucy was not blocked. I hear that they are having a great deal of trouble with the Western trains," remarked sister.

"I don't know what you would have done if you had been kept days in a snow-bank away from your aunties; do you, darling?" said Agnes.

They visited all the large stores, and saw the beautiful Christmas decorations, and purchased lovely, dainty things for Lucy's wardrobe. But she became more and more sober and perplexed. How could Aunt Emma be out shopping, buying things instead of selling them? Why was she not at her glove-counter? Lucy knew quite well the name of the store where her aunt Emma worked. At last they came to it and entered, and then she thought that Aunt Emma would surely remain, go in behind the glove-counter and sell gloves. But sister and Agnes walked straight past the glove-counter. Lucy stopped. She looked hard at the counter. It was a long one, with a number of girls and women. One of them, a middle-aged woman, looked the way she would have imagined her aunt Emma to look had she not been walking with Aunt Emma.

She pulled sister's dress timidly. Sister and Agnes stopped.

"Isn't this where you work, Aunt Emma?" asked little Lucy. Sister and Agnes exchanged glances.

"Yes, dear," replied sister.

"Of course," said Agnes, hurrying along.

"Are you going in behind that counter and sell gloves?" asked little Lucy, with wide, innocent eyes on sister's face.

"Oh yes, of course, dear, very soon," replied sister.

"Very soon," echoed Agnes. "Oh, Lucy darling, look at that beautiful little muff! I think a muff would be sweet for her, sister."

"So it would," cried sister. "Do you want a muff to keep your dear little hands nice and warm, darling?"

"Won't you lose your place if you don't go in behind that counter and sell gloves, Aunt Emma?" persisted little Lucy. "I ain't sick."

"Of course you are not, sweetheart," cried Agnes, hurrying her along. Then she asked the saleslady to tell her the price of muffs.

Sister and Agnes were very glad when they reached home. It had been a sore trial to their nerves and their consciences.

"What do you suppose has put it into her head to call me Aunt Emma, and talk about a glove-counter?" asked sister of Uncle John.

"Who is going to account for the freaks a child that has been allowed to travel all that way alone will take?" he replied, irritably.

The next day was Christmas, and the tree was to be in the afternoon.

"Dr. Jerrold's dear little girl is coming to your Christmas-tree. I know you will love her, darling," said sister.

All that day Lucy was given the most delightful tasks to do; she strung pop-corn, she tied strings to paper angels, she filled candy-bags, she tied ribbons on packages for little Edith Jerrold. She would have been radiantly happy had it not been that the doubts, which had tormented her from the first, grew and grew. Then they reached a climax. Little Lucy had just tied a pink ribbon on a package containing a lovely little gold pin for Edith Jerrold. She had one like it, but that she did not know yet.

"Now, dear," said sister, "can't you print your name on that card to go with it? — Edith, with a Merry Christmas, from Lucy Hooper — this will be your Christmas present to Edith."

Then little Lucy stared blankly at sister, and dropped the package.

"What is it, dear?" asked sister.

"That isn't my name!" said little Lucy, piteously.

Sister and Lucy and Uncle John looked at one another.

"What is your name, darling?" sister asked, faintly.

"Lucy Ames," replied little Lucy.

"Of course it is Lucy Ames," said Uncle John, quickly. He walked off as if he were angry about something, and sister and Agnes both said, "Of course, dear," and she need not write her name on the card, after all; and they gave her a little picture-book to look at, though it was to have been one of her Christmas surprises.

But little Lucy was not quite satisfied. Suddenly she looked intently at sister. "Are you my aunt Emma?" she said.

Sister caught her breath. She looked at Agnes. Then she turned to little Lucy, but her eyes fell before the child's innocent regard. "I am your aunt Alice," she replied. "Not Aunt Emma, but Aunt Alice, darling. You had the name wrong."

"Oh, sister, what made you?" cried Agnes, as she saw the child's face quiver and pale.

"I can't help it," replied sister. "I could not, Agnes, really could not, point-blank. You had the name wrong, darling. It is Aunt Alice whom you have come to live with, and who loves you so much, and not your aunt Emma — not Aunt Emma, but Aunt Alice."

Then poor little Lucy knew. She wailed out with an exceedingly great and bitter cry: "I want my aunt Emma! I want my aunt Emma!"

Uncle John came limping into the room, and when the story had been told him he fibbed unhesitatingly.

"What made you tell Lucy your name was Alice, Emma?" he said, with a half-grin, in spite of his irascibility.

"Oh, John!" sister cried, helplessly.

"You ought to be ashamed of yourself, fibbing so, Emma," said Uncle John. "Why don't you have her put to bed and have a nap?"

"It would be a good idea," said Agnes; "then she can rest before Edith Jerrold comes."

Little Lucy, still sobbing under her breath that she wanted her aunt Emma — for somehow Uncle John had not quite reassured her — was put to bed, but she could not take a nap.

"I know she must be very ill," Agnes said, after she had gone. "Why, John, only just now she had forgotten her name. She said her name was Ames and not Hooper."

"I shall be glad when Frank gets here and looks after her," said Uncle John.

"I don't feel as if I could endure telling such falsehoods much longer," said sister, tearfully.

"I am not sure myself that it is not wise to set her right when she has her name wrong. That is going a little too far," said Uncle John.

"I think so, too," said Agnes.

When little Lucy came down-stairs again they tried, in spite of the doctor's orders, to convince her that her name was Hooper and not Ames. At last they almost succeeded. The child was so docile and bewildered that she almost began to concede that she had been mistaken in her own identity. Finally, when sister asked tenderly if she did not know her name was Lucy Hooper and not Lucy Ames, she replied, in a small, faltering voice:

"Yes, ma'am."

"Oh, she is better," cried sister, in great delight. "You see, it was best to tell the truth. The truth is always best."

"And you know that she is your aunt Alice, and not your aunt Emma, and that she doesn't work at a glove-counter in a store?" asked Agnes.

"Yes, ma'am," said little Lucy.

"She is certainly better," said Agnes.

"Oh, you precious darling, your aunties and your uncle John have been so worried about you!" cried sister; "but now you are almost well again, and we shall all enjoy the Christmas-tree."

The Christmas-tree was very wonderful. Little Edith Jerrold came, and although Lucy was very much afraid of her, she loved her as soon as she saw her. There were presents and presents. Little Lucy was overwhelmed with riches. Her head whirled, and she doubted her identity more than ever. It did not seem as if she could see at all the old self which had been familiar to her small, untrained consciousness. This, more than anything, served to weaken her grasp of old memories. Previously the delusion had all been on the side of the older people; no wit was beginning to infect her.

Poor little Lucy did not for the moment know surely whether she was Lucy Ames or Lucy Hooper, come here to live because her dear mamma was dead and had been the beloved sister of the two ladies and Uncle John, and her papa could not well bring up a little girl, and her papa's parents were very old and feeble. She did not know whether she had come from Brookfield, Massachusetts, or from Cleveland, Ohio; whether she had an Aunt Emma who worked at a glove-counter, or an Aunt Alice who did not work anywhere.

She pondered over the strange problem all the afternoon, even while the presents were being distributed. She could not determine whether they were little Lucy Ames's presents or little Lucy Hooper's.

There was a grand Christmas dinner. Dr. Jerrold came as well as his little daughter. Little Lucy had never seen anything like this dinner, and she had never seen anything like herself as she looked in the mirror when she passed by. It seemed more than ever that she could not be the little Lucy whom she used to see there. She wore a new dress of red silk, and red silk stockings, and red shoes, and red ribbons in her hair, and Aunt Agnes pinned some holly with red berries on her shoulder, and told her she looked like a little Christmas carol.

They had finished dinner, but were still sitting over the nuts and raisins, with their paper bonbon-caps on their heads, when there was a loud ring at the door-bell; then Uncle John was called out, and a great noise of talking was heard in the hall.

Then into the dining-room came Uncle John with a gentleman and a little girl, who did not look unlike Lucy, although she was stouter and not quite so pretty.

Agnes and sister sprang up from the table. "Frank! Frank Hooper! How do you do? We are so glad to —" Then before he could fairly return their greeting they stopped short and stared at the little girl, who looked very sleepy and tired, and had a great smooch of car-smoke across her nose. She rubbed her eyes, and returned the ladies' stare half pitifully and half sulkily.

"Frank," said sister, slowly, "who is this?" She pointed at the little girl.

Agnes stood looking; she seemed speechless.

"Why, that is little Lucy!" replied the rosy-faced gentleman.

Sister and Agnes and Uncle John all turned and pointed at the first little Lucy in a tragic fashion. "No!" said they — "no; *that* is little Lucy."

"I don't know what you mean," returned Mr. Frank Hooper.

"Mean!" cried Uncle John. "Why, it's plain enough what we mean." He pointed again at little Lucy in the red silk frock. "That is your little Lucy!" said Uncle John, severely. "She came here all alone from Cleveland two days ago, and we don't know what you mean when you say *this* is little Lucy. There can't be two little Lucys."

Mr. Frank Hooper laughed and scowled at the same time. "I don't know what *you* mean," said he, eying the first little Lucy sharply. "*This* is *my* little Lucy, and though she started last Sunday, she has just fetched up here on the same train with me. Her train was stalled in the snow, and some people took her off and took care of her, and, as luck would have it, put her on my train. I don't know what it all means. I don't know why you telegraphed me that Lucy was sick. She wasn't sick, and if she had been, how would you have known? I'm the one who would like to know the meaning of it."

"Who is that child over there?" demanded Uncle John, pointing to little Lucy.

Sister went close to her and pulled the little yellow head down on her shoulder. "She's a darling, whoever she is," she declared, half weeping.

"I don't know who she is," declared Mr. Frank Hooper. "I never saw her before."

"And she isn't your little girl?"

"I tell you no. Here is my little girl. What in creation is the matter with you all?" At that juncture the second little Lucy began to cry, and Agnes caught her up peremptorily.

"Poor child," she said, "she is all tired out and hungry."

"I expect she is," said Mr. Frank Hooper, shortly.

"There, dear, don't cry," said Agnes, pulling off the second little Lucy's hat and coat. "You shall have your dinner right away."

"Who is that child?" asked Uncle John, vaguely pointing at the first Lucy.

Then Dr. Jerrold came forward. "I think there is a grave mistake here," he said, "and I think I am partly to blame." Then he turned to the first Lucy. "What is your name, my dear?" he said. "Speak up; don't be afraid; nobody is going to hurt you."

"I rather think nobody *will* hurt her," said sister, kissing her.

"What is your name, dear?" asked Uncle John.

"Little Lucy."

"Your whole name?" said the doctor.

"Lucy Ames," little Lucy sobbed out.

"That is what she has said all along," said sister.

"And where were you going?" asked Dr. Jerrold.

"To Boston to see my aunt Emma," replied little Lucy.

"And where was your aunt Emma in Boston?"

"She worked at the glove-counter in Gibbs & Simkins's store," sobbed Lucy.

"And where did you come from?"

"From Brookfield, Massachusetts."

"That is what the dear little thing has kept saying from the very first, and we would not listen to her," said sister, fairly sobbing herself. "I call it a shame. We ought to have believed her."

"It was my fault," said Dr. Jerrold, "but I assumed that you knew."

"We acted like a parcel of opinionated idiots," growled Uncle John. "I don't know that you were to blame, doctor. I'm inclined to think *other* people were to blame. Children ought not to be let to travel alone, anyway." Uncle John glared accusingly at Mr. Frank Hooper, who did not seem to notice it.

"But," said Dr. Jerrold, "what is this Aunt Emma doing all this time?"

Then Agnes and sister and Uncle John all jumped up at once.

"What is your aunt Emma's last name, dear?" inquired the doctor.

"Aunt Emma Avery," replied little Lucy.

"She knew all about it all this time, and here she was dragged in here, whether or no," said sister, tearfully. "Don't you be afraid, darling."

Uncle John rang the bell violently. "Well," he said, "that woman shall not be kept waiting a moment longer than can be helped. I'll have the carriage out, and I'll find her. The janitor at Gibbs & Simkins will know." But it was Dr. Jerrold and Agnes who finally went, on account of Uncle John's rheumatism.

They were not gone very long. It was hardly three-quarters of an hour before the carriage stopped before the house and the front door opened. The family were all in the great drawing-room where the Christmas-tree stood. Sister was holding the first little Lucy in her lap and comforting her; Mr. Hooper was holding the second little Lucy, who had eaten her dinner, had her face washed, and looked happier. Now and then she and the first Lucy smiled shyly at each other. Uncle John and Mr. Hooper had been talking rather excitedly, but they hushed when the carriage stopped, and Mr. Hooper, who was somewhat impetuous, jumped up and ran to the drawing-room door. Then Dr. Jerrold and Agnes and a pale but very pretty woman in a black dress, who was Aunt Emma, and old Lysander and Sylvia entered.

Old Lysander saw little Lucy, and he went straight to her, and she slid down from sister's lap.

"Oh, grandpa! grandpa!" she sobbed out.

Then old Lysander caught her up in his arms. Sylvia was crying very softly and unobtrusively, with her nicely folded best pocket-handkerchief pressed to her face. Aunt Emma was trying not to cry, and trying to respond politely to Agnes's and sister's agitated apologies and explanations. As for old Lysander, he fairly shook little Lucy in his joy.

"Grandpa's ducky darlin'," he said, huskily. "Did she get lost, and not know where she was? And here's poor Aunt Emma been almost crazy, and it all happened because it snowed so hard the night little Lucy came, and made Aunt Emma's car late. And poor Aunt Emma sent for grandpa and grandma, and here they be."

Finally, after much explanation and an amiable under-standing, little Lucy was taken away in the carriage with her grandfather and grandmother and her aunt Emma to her aunt Emma's boarding-place. She stayed there three days, and the boarders gave her a little Christmas-tree, and one lady took her to see "Cinderella." Then sister and Agnes and the other little Lucy came to see her, and they all went to see "Jack and the Bean-stalk," and she went happily through all her aunt Emma's promised list of Christmas joys, with the additional joy of her grandparents' society.

On the Monday after Christmas, old Lysander and Sylvia and little Lucy all returned home to Brookfield. The next morning they were all in the kitchen keeping Christmas, though Christmas was several days old. Old Lysander said that they had not had their Christmas at home yet, and little Lucy had not received the presents which he had purchased at Ebbit's store. So that morning they were given to her, and that made the third set of Christmas presents.

"Three Christmases in one year, ain't it, ducky darlin'?" said old Lysander. He himself had some very nice presents from Aunt Emma and sister and Agnes and Uncle John, and so had Sylvia. It was still very bitter weather, but clear and bright. The frosted window-panes shone like the pages of a missal, with the tints of jewels on leaves of silver. Sylvia was stirring something on the stove, which gave forth a sweet and spicy odor. Little Lucy sat in her tiny rocking-chair, with her arms full of dolls. She sat in the midst of incalculable riches of childhood, her face radiant with the utmost joy of possession, borne with the gentleness and gratitude of a gentle little girl. Old Lysander was in his arm-chair near her. The kitchen windows faced southeast, and soon the frost began to melt.

The sun shone broadly in athwart the yellow-painted floor; old Lysander and little Lucy, the good old man and the good child, at the close and beginning of innocent and peaceful lives, sat in the same beam of Christmas sunshine.

EGLANTINA

"Eglantina, tall and fair,
Queen of Beauty and of Grace,
All my darkened house of life
Is illumined by thy face.

"Shineth thou unto my heart
As the dew in morning field,
When beneath the eastern sun
Gems of Zion blaze revealed.

"Sweet'nest thou my every thought
Like the bud when night hath passed,
And she breaks her seal of bloom
To become a rose at last.

"Though in gloom thy lover sighs,
Eglantina, tall and fair,
Love the Blind hath touched his eyes,
And he sees thee past compare."

These verses abounding in conceits, and appealing to the purely personal rather than to the broadly human side of love and tender sentiment, were cut and skilfully colored, illuminated after a simple fashion, on a window-shutter in the east parlor of the old Litchfield house, in Litchfield Village. The furniture of the east parlor was after the fashion of Queen Anne. There were bulky-drawered pieces rearing themselves with precarious grace on tall, slim, and fragile legs; there were tables which seemed to have a perpetual swaying motion of their own, the ornaments whereon — the shells and china vases and card-baskets — faintly jingled when one crossed the room; there were sofas and chairs which creaked with faint remonstrance but never succumbed under weight. The sofas and chairs had been upholstered with sea-green, then it faded to a green like a dim reminiscence of the color which might have served as a background for memories of old bloom — the long-past roses and pinks and heartsease of old gardens, of the old garden behind the Litchfield house, and, if one chose to think further, of the youthful joys of the dwellers in the house.

That was Eglantina's favorite room, and there she used to sit with Roger Proctor. Eglantina's father had married for the second time when her mother had been dead ten years and she was eleven. The new wife had been a widow with one child, Roger Proctor, a year younger than Eglantina. Dr. Eliphalet Litchfield had been jealous of this son by a former husband, and had insisted upon the mother's practically separating from him upon her marriage with himself.

So the boy, who had been blind from scarlet-fever ever since his infancy, was put to board with a distant relative of his mother's, and was seldom seen by her.

Dr. Eliphalet Litchfield was a man of such concentrated tenderness towards a few that it gave rise to cruelty towards others. All his life he had also been suspicious of that which he loved, lest it not belong wholly and unreservedly to him, and he fought for his own against the phantoms of his brain and not against real foes. Although he always feared that she did not, the new wife easily loved him better than she loved her blind son, for Dr. Litchfield was a personable and masterful man, who could compel, although long past youth, almost any woman to his will. The new wife was scarcely more than a girl, although a widow with a son of ten. She was a mild and delicate creature, whose only force of character lay in loving devotion, and that proved too strenuous for her fragile constitution. She died a year after her marriage, and her little daughter died with her.

Then Dr. Litchfield sent for the blind son of the dead woman, and lavished upon him a curious affection, which was at first not so much affection as a sentiment of duty and remorse. This man, given to fierce strains of mood, chose to fancy that his young wife's untimely death was to be held in the light of a judgment of God for their desertion of her blind son. He never looked in the boy's sightless face without seeing that of a long-since-dead but nevertheless triumphant rival, and he saw also, in the boy himself, another aspirant, and a rightful one, to his lost wife's love; but he was devoted to his welfare. From the time that Roger Proctor came to live in the Litchfield house his lines were cast in pleasant places. Dr. Litchfield enjoined upon his daughter Eglantina that she was to treat the strange little boy as her own brother, and he himself showed more indulgence towards him than towards her. Roger, although a boy, and blind, went clad in finer raiment than Eglantina; he had a pony and rode when she walked. He was taught by expensive teachers, while Eglantina had to be satisfied with simpler and less expensive instruction, for Dr. Litchfield was not a rich man. Roger had the best bedroom in the house, and

Eglantina a small one, hot in summer and cold in winter. Had the girl anything she loved for which the boy expressed a preference, she was straightway reminded that she must give it up cheerfully to her blind brother. However, Eglantina needed no such reminding. From the minute that the blind child entered the house the other child was his willing slave. Nothing was ever seen more appealing to old and young than that little blind boy, Roger Proctor. His hair, which hung in straight, smooth lengths, had a wonderful high light around his head which suggested an aureole. His young face, between these lines of gold, was an oval so pure that it had an effect of majesty and peace even in the child. His blind eyes, large and blue, seeming to give instead of receive light, gazed with unswerving directness from under a high forehead of innocent seriousness. Although his forehead seemed almost frowning with gravity, Roger's mouth was always smiling with a wonderful smile, before which people shrank a little. "He looks like an angel," they said. It was a smile of inward cognizance rather than observation, and revealed, as nothing else could have done, the nature of the boy. It gave evidence of the estimation in which a perfectly simple and guileless soul held those around him who appealed to his crippled senses. There was that about the boy which excited a certain fear and awe. His was a most perfect limpidity of nature. One looking therein saw everything — reflections and depths of innocence. His motives shone through all his actions with unmistakable radiance. The blind boy gave, as no seeing child could have done, an impression of light and clearness. Soon his step-father adored him, and as for Eglantina, she worshipped him from the first. No greater contrast could have been imagined than there was between the girl and the boy. They were of about the same age, but Eglantina was head and shoulders above Roger, though he was not below the usual height. But Eglantina was abnormally tall; her stature was almost a deformity, especially since she was exceedingly slender. And that was not all. Crowning that slim height was a head and face unfortunate not so much from lack of beauty as from a mark on one cheek which had been there from birth. A story was told in the village of how Dr. Litchfield's wife had longed for roses in winter when there were none, and talked of the rose which climbed over the front porch in the summer-time, and declared that she could smell them when none were there, and how at last when Eglantina was born, there on one little cheek was that hideous travesty of a red rose which she must bear until the day of her death. The mother, who had a strong vein of romance, had called the child Eglantina, and mourned until she died, not long after, because of her disfigurement, and often kissed with tears of self-reproach and the most passionate tenderness and pity the mark on the little cheek, as if she would kiss it away.

Dr. Litchfield ever after hated roses; he would have none in his garden, and the eglantine over the front porch was rooted up. Eglantina herself had an antipathy to roses, and never could she have a whiff of rose-scent unless she turned faint and ill. Nothing could exceed the child's sensitiveness with regard to the mark on her cheek. She never looked in her glass without seeing that, and that only. That dreadful blur of youth and beauty seemed all her face; she was blind to all else. She shrank from strangers with a shyness that was almost panic. Eyes upon her face seemed to scorch her very heart. But as she grew older, although the inward suffering was much the same, she learned to give less outward evidence of it. She no longer shrank so involuntarily from strangers; she even endured pitying glances, or repulsion, with a certain gentleness which gave evidence of enormous patience rather than bravery. When Roger had been in her father's house some years, she became conscious of a feeling which filled her with horror. She strove against it, she tried to imagine that it was not so, that she could not be such a monster, but she knew all of a sudden that she was glad that Roger was blind. Whenever she looked at him came the wild, selfish triumph and joy that he could not see her. Her consciousness of this came upon her in full force for the first time one afternoon in August, when she was eighteen and Roger a few months younger. They were crossing a field behind the house, hand-in-hand as usual, for, although Roger could walk very well alone, he moved with more certainty — and that not alone from his lack of sight, but from the lack of something in his nature — if he were in leading of some one. Eglantina was still much taller. They strolled together across the wide field sloping to the south. The field was rosy with sorrel, out of which flew butterflies of much the same color with a curious effect as if the flowers themselves had taken wings. Eglantina told Roger. "The butterflies fly up in clouds, and it looks as if the flowers themselves had broken loose from the ground; they are of the same color," said she.

Roger turned his sightless eyes towards the sorrel, and nodded and smiled as if he saw. "I have made a poem to you, Eglantina," said he.

Eglantina colored until the rest of her face was as red as the rose-mark on her left cheek, then she turned pale, and that brought it into stronger relief. "You must not," she said, faintly.

"Why not? There is no one in the whole world as beautiful as you are, Eglantina."

"No, I am not," she returned, in a pitiful, hesitating voice, as if the truth were stifling her.

"Yes."

"You do not know; you never saw me."

"I have seen you with my whole soul. You are the most beautiful girl in the whole world, Eglantina."

Eglantina shut her mouth hard. She pulled her broad-brimmed hat over her face by the green bridle-ribbon, and cast her disfigured cheek into a deep shadow.

It was a burning day, the ground was hot to their feet, perfumed waves of steaming air came in their faces. There was a loud din of locusts. Over in another field some men were mowing, swinging their scythes in glittering circles, and now and then calling to one another with hoarse laughter. Then came the liquid call of a quail, then shouts of children over in the road. It seemed to Eglantina as if the whole world was in a merry dance of love and progress, and that she alone was caught motionless in the current of fate.

Roger looked at her anxiously. "What is the matter, Eglantina?" he asked, softly.

"Nothing," said she.

When they reached home, she ran up to her own chamber. She went to her little mirror over her white-draped dressing-table and gazed long in it. Then she sank down before it on the floor in an agony of self-abasement. After a while she rose and pulled the muslin drapery over the glass, and did not look in it again. When she went down-stairs there was Roger's poem cut skilfully on the shutter in the east parlor. Roger could not use pen or pencil to much advantage, but he could cut the letters plainly, feeling them with his long, sensitive fingers. Eglantina held her cambric pocket-handkerchief over her marred cheek and read every word, smiling tenderly. Then she put the handkerchief to her eyes and leaned against the shutter and sobbed softly. Then Roger came into the room, feeling his way towards her, and she choked her sobs back and dried her eyes. Roger wished to color the letters of his poem, and Eglantina sorted out the colors from her paint-box, and he painted them.

Then every time that she saw that poem to Eglantina, tall and fair, she tried to picture herself as Roger saw her, and not as she really was. She tried to forget the birth-mark, she tried not to think of it when she spoke to Roger, lest the consciousness of it be evident in her voice, but that she could not compass. She thought of it always, and the more she strove against it the more she was conscious of it, until she grew to feel as if the mark were on her very soul.

But her patience grew and grew to keep pace with it. Eglantina had been an impatient child, nervous and irritable, but all that had gone. There were in her heart ceaseless torture and suffering, but never rebellion. She thought of the mark as her shame and her fault; she unreasoningly reproached herself because of it, but she never complained of her hard fate.

Everybody who knew Eglantina spoke well of her. They said what a pity that such a good girl should be under such an affliction, and they also said when they saw the piteous couple together — the man who could not see and the woman who should not be seen — that there was an ideal match. Eglantina's father began also to have that fancy. He had grown old of late years, and had the troubled persistency of a child for his way, when once he had begun to dwell upon it. It was not long after Roger had cut his verses to Eglantina, tall and fair, on the shutter. The old man spied them one afternoon when he had returned from a call in the village, for his professional services were still in demand. The shutter had swung into the room in a sudden gust of east wind, and he had caught sight of something unwonted upon it. He put on his glasses and stood close to the shutter, reading laboriously. That evening he called Eglantina back after she had started up-stairs with her candle. "Eglantina, come here a moment," he said, "I want to speak to you."

Eglantina returned and stood before him, the candle-light illuminating her poor face, which her father had never seen without a qualm of pain and rebellion. That mark was for him like a blot on the fair face of love itself, and his will rose up against it in futile revolt.

Her father looked at her, his forehead contracted, then he turned towards the shutter, and again towards her with a half-smile, while one long finger pointed to the verses. "Have you seen these, Eglantina?" he said.

"Yes, sir," replied Eglantina, gravely. She looked full at her father with a look which was fairly eloquent. "See what I am," it said. "What have I to do with love-verses? Why do you mock me by speaking of this?"

But her father shook his head stubbornly as if in direct answer to such unspoken speech of hers. "If," he said, with a sort of stern abashedness, for he had never spoken of such things to his daughter — "if your own heart leads you in that direction, Eglantina, there is no possible objection, and I should like to see you settled. I am growing old."

Eglantina, still speechless, raised one arm, her lace sleeve falling back from her wrist, and pointed to her marred left cheek. There was in the gesture utmost resignation and pride, and her eyes reproved her father mutely.

Her father frowned and continued shaking his head in denial. "I still say that under the circumstances there can be no possible objection," he said. "What difference can that make to a blind man, who has learned to esteem you for your own true worth, and has invested you in his own mind with the graces of person to correspond with those of your character?"

Eglantina looked at him. After all, she was eager to be persuaded. "I cannot keep it secret from him," she faltered.

"How can you do aught else? How can you describe your face to a blind man?"

Eglantina continued to regard her father with eyes of painful searching, as one who would discover hope against conviction and find refutation for her own argument.

"Roger has been told repeatedly," said her father.

Eglantina nodded. She herself had told him, and he had laughed at her.

"And the telling conveys no meaning to him," said her father. "What does beauty or deformity of the flesh signify to a blind man?"

"I can see, and I can see that which he loves mistakenly," replied Eglantina, in a pitiful voice.

The two stood facing each other, both the father and daughter above middle height, for Eglantina got her height from her father. The two faces were on a level — Dr. Litchfield's, thin to asceticism, domed by a high, bald forehead, confronted the other face illuminated by the upward gleam of the candle, and his lightened unexpectedly with surprise and approbation. The east wind, salt with the sea, came in at the open window. The girl's white gown wound around her in ruffling folds, for the window was at her back; her brown hair, which was long and fine and curling, blew over her disfigured cheek, partly concealing it. That of her face which was visible was not unpleasing, though irregular, being too full of curves, even her profile having no clearly cut lines. Eglantina's face gave the impression of a sweet dissonance of overlapping curves, and suggested a rose. Moreover, under the upward light of the candle, it took on, as to lips and eyes, a radiant sparkle of dewy youth. She looked fairly beautiful to her father. For the first time the girl saw a look of admiration fixed upon her poor face. "You are not so bad-looking, after all, my child," her father said, in a new voice, and Eglantina's heart leaped, and for the minute she was actually beautiful. She was triumphant over her deformity.

"Do as your heart dictates, my daughter," said her father, "and have no fear."

Eglantina pulled her hair farther over the disfigured cheek; she looked at her father with a smile at once foolish, doubtful, and beatific, then she turned without a word and went out with white robes and brown hair streaming back, and her candle was extinguished in the draught as she passed the door.

The next day, in the afternoon, she was seated in the arbor in the garden with her embroidery work. She worked cunning eyelet holes in a strip of linen, and the shadow of the vines made a soft, green gloom in the place, and near by was a hive of bees, and she could hear their drowsy hum and see their winged flights to a great bed of pinks, wilting in the full blaze of the sunlight, and giving out a great, panting fragrance of spice and honey. There were no roses in the garden, and there were virgin's-bower and a hop-vine over the arbor, instead of the eglantine which had formerly shaded it.

Presently Eglantina saw Roger coming, walking almost as if he saw, with no outstretching of feeling hands. In fact, he knew his way well enough between the flower-beds, being guided by their various odors. His direct path to Eglantina in the arbor lay between mignonette and pinks on one side and sweet alyssum and thyme on the other.

Eglantina, watching him approach, swept a great bunch of brown curls completely over her disfigured cheek, and sat so when he entered.

"Pass all the other lesser flowers by until you find the rose," he said, laughing tenderly.

"I am no rose," said Eglantina.

"The rose does not know she is herself, else she would be no rose," said Roger.

"I am a poor mockery of a rose, from this dreadful mark on my cheek," said Eglantina, and she felt as if she were about to die, for it seemed to her that such brutal frankness must convince.

But Roger only laughed. "The rose has a scratch from a thorn on one of her petals," he returned, "or a bee has sucked too greedily for honey. What of it? Is there not enough beauty left?

There is no one in the whole world so beautiful as you, Eglantina. A mark on your cheek! What is a mark on your cheek but a beauty, since it is a part of you? Fret no more about it, sweetheart."

Eglantina looked at him, at the beautiful face in a cloud of golden beard, at the sightless blue eyes, and she pulled the curls closer over her cheek and resisted no longer.

It was then the 1st of September, and it was decided to have the marriage the next month — there was no reason why they should wait, and Dr. Litchfield was disposed to hasten the wedding. Soon the simple preparations were nearly finished. Roger's chamber had been newly papered with a pale-green satin paper, sprinkled with bouquets of flowers. Roger's wedding-suit was ready and Eglantina's gown. The gown was a peach-blow silk, and it lay in shimmering folds on the high bed in the spare chamber, and from the tester floated the veil, and a pair of little rose-colored slippers toed out daintily beside the dimity dressing-table, and in a little box thereon was a brooch which Roger had given her — a knot of his fair hair set in a circle of pearls.

The summer was still fervid. One evening, after a very warm day, Roger and Eglantina had been walking a long way down the country road towards the village, and it was late when they returned and went into the house. The moon was long risen and the dew was heavy, like a hoar-frost over the meadows and gardens, and all things sweetened in it. There was a great breath of rowen hay over the land, and of wild grapes and apples and pears. Now and then came a dark flap of a wing of mystery, and a whip-poorwill called out of the willows on the border of a brook.

Roger and Eglantina kissed each other in the front entry, then Roger went up-stairs, in the dark and Eglantina lighted her chamber candle.

But her father called her again, and she went into the east parlor as before, with the candle throwing an upward light upon her face. This time Dr. Litchfield hesitated long before speaking, so long that she looked at him in surprise, thinking that she had, perhaps, not understood and he had not called her. "Did you want to see me, father?" she asked.

"Yes, Eglantina," he replied, but still he hesitated, and she waited in growing wonder and alarm.

"Eglantina," Dr. Litchfield said, presently.

"Yes, father."

"Dr. David Lyman is in the south village. He has been attending the daughter of Squire Eggleston, who lost her sight from scarlet-fever," her father said, abruptly.

Eglantina turned white and gave a quick gasp.

"He will restore her sight," said her father, "and —" he paused. Eglantina was silent and motionless. She stood with her mouth set hard and her eyes averted.

"It might be well to have him see Roger," said her father. He did not look at her.

Eglantina turned and went out of the room without a word.

That night she did not sleep. She was awake all night, pleading pitilessly for and against herself, as if she had been a stranger. Monstrous as it might seem, there was something to be said in favor of letting the physician who might restore Roger's sight pass by and keeping her lover blind until the day of his death. Eglantina, reflecting impartially, knew quite well that if it were her own case, and she had to choose between love and sight, what she should do. "If Roger gains his sight he loses love," she said. "And he is one who, if love go amiss, will come to harm in himself." And that was quite true, for Roger Proctor was a man to be made or marred by love, for he lacked that in his character which would make him stand or fall unto himself alone.

"Will he not lose more than he gains?" Eglantina asked herself, and though her judgment told her yes, yet she dared not trust to her judgment when her inclination so swayed her. Then, moreover, to such strength her love had grown that all the old, guilty, secret gladness over his blindness was gone, and instead was a great tenderness and pity for her lover that he must go blind and miss so much. "He can see a plenty that is beautiful if he miss the beauty in me," thought Eglantina; "and who am I to say that no other woman besides me can make him happy?"

But always she went back to the fear as to how he would endure the awful shock when, after his eyesight was restored, he should look for the first time on her face and see what he had loved and kissed. She thought truly not then of her own distress and humiliation, but of him, and what he would suffer, and she could not argue that away. Then all at once her mind was at rest, for a great and unselfish, though fantastic, plan had occurred to her, and she knew what she could do to spare him.

The next morning her father looked at her, and looked again as if to be sure he saw aright, for he did not seem to see the birthmark at all. There was a strange expression in her face which dominated all disfigurement, and would have dominated beauty as well.

"When will he come?" she asked her father, when Roger was not within hearing.

"This afternoon if I go for him," replied her father, with his eyes still on her face; "but you had best not tell Roger until the doctor has pronounced on the case. You had best not hold up hope that may come to naught."

"It will not come to naught," she replied, and after breakfast she told Roger that a doctor was coming who would cure his eyes and he would see.

Roger received the news with a curious calmness at first, but as he reflected a great joy grew and strengthened in his face. Then he cried out, suddenly, "Then I shall see you; I shall see you!"

"Yes," said Eglantina.

"Why do you speak so, Eglantina? Your voice sounds strange." There was a peculiar quality in Eglantina's voice, a peculiarity of intonation which made it unmistakable among others, and just then it had disappeared.

"Why strange?" said she.

"It is strange now. Are you not glad that I am to see — to see you, sweetheart?"

"I am more than glad," replied Eglantina. Then she went away hurriedly, though Roger called wonderingly and in a hurt fashion after her.

That afternoon before the doctor came Eglantina sent a letter to her cousin Charlotte Wyatt, who lived in Boston, and who was to be present at the wedding, to hasten her coming. The two were great friends, though Charlotte had visited Eglantina but once, when Roger was away, and so had never seen him; but Eglantina had often visited Boston, and the two wrote frequent letters.

"Come if you can in a fortnight's time, dear Charlotte," wrote Eglantina, "though that be a fortnight before the day set for the wedding, for I am in sore trouble and distress of mind, and only you can comfort and help me." And she wrote not a word with regard to Roger's eyes. And she did not mention Charlotte's coming to Roger.

That afternoon Dr. David Lyman came at Dr. Litchfield's bidding, and the operation on Roger's eyes was performed with great hope of success, though the result could not be certainly known for the space of two weeks, when the bandages should be removed and Dr. Lyman would return. During those two weeks Eglantina nursed Roger tenderly and let no trace of her own sadness appear. Indeed, she began to feel that she should have joy enough if Roger regained his sight, even if she lost him thereby, for the blind man was full of delight, and for the first time revealed how he had suffered in his mind because of his loss of sight.

Then the day before the one appointed for the removing of the bandages came Charlotte Wyatt, stepping out of the stage-coach at the door, a tall and most beautiful and stately maiden, who was held in great renown for her beauty, being called the beautiful Charlotte Wyatt, and being the toast of all the young men and sought in marriage by many. Charlotte Wyatt, with all her beauty, bore a certain family resemblance to her cousin. She was of the same height, she was shaped like her, she moved and spoke like her, having the same trick of intonation in her grave, sweet voice. But this resemblance only served to make Eglantina's defects a more lamentable contrast to the other's beauty. It was like a perfect and a deformed rose on the same bush. The deformed flower was the worse deformed for being a rose beside the other.

That night the two girls lay awake all night in bed and talked, and Eglantina told the other her trouble, and yet not all, for she did not discover to her the plan which she had made. Charlotte held her cousin in her arms and wept over her, and pitied her with a pity which bore a cruel sting in it. "I do not wonder that your heart aches, sweetheart, for surely never was a man like Roger, and you might well love him better blind than any other man with his sight," said Charlotte Wyatt, fervently. She had not spoken to Roger, but she had peeped into the room where he sat with his eyes bandaged, with Eglantina reading to him. Eglantina shrank from her suddenly when she said that. "What is the matter? What have I said to hurt you, sweet?" cried Charlotte.

"Nothing, dear," replied Eglantina, and held the other girl close in her arms as they lay in bed.

"I never loved any man overmuch, though so many have said that they loved me, but I can see how you love Roger," Charlotte said, innocently.

"There is no one like him," Eglantina agreed, and she began sobbing in a despairing fashion, and Charlotte strove to comfort her. "He will love you just the same when he can see," she said. "Beauty is but skin deep, sweetheart."

"I care not — oh, I care not, so he is not hurt," sobbed Eglantina.

"How you love him!" whispered the other girl. "If he is not true to love like yours, he is more blind when he sees than when he saw not."

"No, he will not be one whit to blame," cried Eglantina, angrily. She sprang out of bed and ran to her looking-glass, and she looked in it, and the candle was burning at the side, and she saw her face plainly, and Charlotte also saw it in the glass. Then Eglantina turned and looked at her cousin, and Charlotte's eyes fell. "Oh, Eglantina, I — I wish —" she began, brokenly. Then she wept aloud for pity and confusion. "I will always love you. Your face is beautiful to me. I will always love you," she sobbed, and it was the same as if she had owned that Roger would not.

It was the next afternoon that the bandages were to be removed from Roger Proctor's eyes, and it would then be known if the operation were a success. The great doctor and Eglantina's father and the nurse were in the room with Roger. Eglantina and Charlotte waited outside. Charlotte was dressed in a lilac satin gown falling in soft folds around her lovely height, and her fair hair was twisted into a great knot from which fell a shower of loose curls around her rosy face, and since she had come away without a certain tucker of wrought lace which she much affected, Eglantina had dressed her in one of her own, taking it from a drawer where it had lain with a sachet of lavender, and she had fastened it with her brooch of Roger's hair set in pearls.

The two moved up and down; neither could rest, for an uneasiness as great as Eglantina's was apparently over the other girl. The girls of the same height, with the same fashion of wearing their hair, with the same tricks of motion, with the lamentable difference of likeness in their faces, seemed to fill all the east parlor with the same fluttering wind of agitation. Charlotte espied the verses to "Eglantina, tall and fair" on the shutter, and began to read them aloud, then paused for shame and confusion before she said 'fair,' and Eglantina listened unmoved. Then Charlotte ran to her and laid her beautiful, rosy cheek against her cousin's disfigured one and kissed her, and the kiss seemed to burn Eglantina, but she did not shrink.

They listened to every sound from the next room, the doctor's study, where Roger and the two physicians were, and presently out came Dr. Eliphalet Litchfield, not with the gladness of his profession after a successful operation, but falteringly, with pitiful eyes upon his daughter.

"Well?" said Eglantina to him.

"He sees," replied Dr. Litchfield, in a husky voice. He looked hesitatingly at Eglantina. The door of the next room was opened again, and Dr. David Lyman looked out. "He is asking for your daughter," he said to Eliphalet Litchfield, and after a swift glance at Eglantina he fastened his gaze upon Charlotte. He had seen neither before, Eglantina having kept herself out of his sight, and he thought Charlotte was she.

"Eglantina, Eglantina," called Roger's voice, high with nervousness, from the next room. He was too weak to stir; the strain had been severe, and he was of a delicate physique. "You had best come at once," whispered Dr. David Lyman, who was a small, fair man with a manner of imperious incisiveness, to Charlotte. "He has been under a great stress, and it is not advisable to cross him; even his sight may depend upon it." Then he turned impatiently to Dr. Litchfield. "Your daughter had better come," he said.

Before Charlotte could speak, Eglantina laid a hand with a weight of steel on her arm. "Go," she said.

Charlotte stared at her, pale and scared.

"Go," said Eglantina.

Dr. Litchfield made a motion forward, but Eglantina stopped him with a look. She pushed Charlotte towards the study door, and whispered sharply in her ear. "You heard what the doctor said," she whispered. "Don't let him know. Go."

Charlotte went into the room, half by force, half with bewildered quiescence. Then the three outside heard a great cry of rapture from Roger.

Eglantina went away hurriedly. The two men stood looking at each other. "She is my daughter," said Dr. Eliphalet Litchfield.

"My God," said the other.

It was nearly time for the stage-coach to pass the house. Eglantina was waiting for it at the turn of the road beyond. She wore her long green cloak and carried a bandbox. No one had seen her leave the house. An hour later Dr. Litchfield found a letter pinned to his cloak, which hung in the entry. It was very brief:

> "Dear father, — this is to inform you that I have gone to Aunt Pamela's. Do not undeceive Roger at present, and do not let Charlotte. Your respectful and obedient daughter to command,
> "Eglantina."

Eglantina's aunt Pamela Litchfield lived in the next village of Stonybrook. She was a maiden woman with a large estate, and she lived alone, with the exception of one old servant. When her niece arrived and told her story, or a great part of her story, she listened with amazement and a large mixture of admiration and sympathy. A considerable vein of romance had this old maiden lady, although she held it for the most part well in check, and was considered to have disdained many good opportunities for matrimony.

"And do you propose that your father and cousin should continue this deception long, my dear?" she said.

"As long as may be needful," replied Eglantina.

"Until Roger falls in love with Charlotte?" asked the old lady, shrewdly.

"He is in love with her now."

"Because he thinks Charlotte Eglantina."

"She is the Eglantina whom he loved."

"Nonsense, dear child; she is not the Eglantina whom he loved, unless 'twas a surface affection not worthy the name of love."

"He could not love a face like mine," said Eglantina, gently and proudly.

"Think you that your father and cousin will consent to such deceit?"

"They must until he is recovered."

"And when they tell him, what then?"

"Then he will love Charlotte, and she will love him, and all will be well."

"All will not be well," said Pamela Litchfield, firmly. But she said no more; she coaxed her niece to eat, and by-and-by to sleep, after a composing draught of orange-flower water. Next morning she sent a letter to her brother, but she kept Eglantina, and let no one see her, and tended her, and made much of her, secretly adoring her as a heroine who had done a noble and unheard-of deed for love. Eglantina had been with her Aunt Pamela a week, when one afternoon came Charlotte, riding in the doctor's chaise, herself driving with a pretty skill, holding the reins high, slapping the white horse's back with them, and clucking to him like a bird to hasten his pace. And she, running into Miss Pamela Litchfield's house, and finding Eglantina by herself embroidering in the parlor, in the deep window-seat, caught her round the waist, and talked fast, half laughing and half crying. "He will not have me," she said. "He yet believes me to be you, though my conscience chides me sore for the deceit. Your father has been silent, too, though 'twas against his will; yet what could we do, since you left us in such a plaguy lurch, and Dr. Lyman saying he must not be crossed. But he will have none of me, and this morning he told me, with as near tears as a man may, that he accounted himself as worthy of great blame, but held that he might be worthy of more did he dissemble. Then did my pretty gentleman inform me — me, Charlotte Wyatt, that his feelings had changed, that he held himself in great despite for the change, and considered that in gaining his sight he had lost that which was infinitely more precious, and also his good esteem for himself, but he saw nothing for it but the truth, though sorely troubled to speak it. This to me, and to my uncle, your father, he said more. This he said of me, of me who has had some praise, whether deserved or not, for her looks, and hath been sought of many men with eyesight of the best — that he was disappointed in my poor face, that it was not what he had deemed it to be, that it was less fair. Nay, he even went further, this blind man who now sees, and called it, not hideous, for he is too gentle a man for that, but he admitted that it hath a repulsion for his fastidiousness. And then I, having heard what he said to my uncle, and being, I will admit, something taken aback by such slighting, must needs march in and tell this particular gentleman, Roger Proctor, the truth, or at least a part of the truth, for your magnanimity I kept from him, for I began to have an inkling that he would be sorely hurt instead of pleased by it. I told him that it was all a deception, that I was my poor self instead of his beloved Eglantina, that she had been unexpectedly called away, and that we had deceived him for his health's sake, and, Lord! had you but seen how he brightened! And now you must go to him, sweetheart."

But Eglantina at that lost all the firmness which had sustained her, and wept and implored, and declared that she could not, but Charlotte and Pamela Litchfield pleaded with her, and comforted and encouraged her, Charlotte saying that it was considered highly dangerous even yet for Roger to be thwarted in any way, since he was exceeding nervous, and a mental strain might bring about inflammation to the eyes, and finally she yielded.

It was evening when Eglantina and Charlotte, in the doctor's chaise, rode into the yard of the Litchfield house, and Eglantina did not see Roger until the next morning. In the morning she went into the east parlor where he sat. She opened the door abruptly, for she had no courage for delay, and entered, and stood before Roger Proctor, and a sunbeam from the east window, the lettered shutter of which had been thrown open, fell upon her poor face with the monstrous travesty of a rose disfiguring her cheek, and Roger gave one great, glad cry of recognition, and she was in his arms, and he was covering her face with kisses, and looking at it with ecstasy, as if it were the face of an angel. "Oh, Eglantina," he said. "It is you, sweetheart, you and no other; no other could have such beauty as thine, the beauty I have seen with my soul and now see with my twice-blessed eyes."

For, strange as it may seem, this poor Eglantina seemed to Roger Proctor more beautiful than one of the greatest beauties of her day. It may have been from a false standard of taste, or he may have been always blinded by love, even after he had gained his sight, or, as some held, it may have been that the mark on Eglantina's face had in some way so chastened and influenced her character of humility and patience and unselfishness that a harmony deeper and truer than any ordinary loveliness had been established between her affliction and her soul, and she had become in a high and spiritual sense a beauty, indeed, to those who might be able to see.

Eglantina lived and died, and her long grave is in the grave-yard of Litchfield Village, and at the head is a marble stone on which are cut the verses beginning, "Eglantina, tall and fair."

They who read may well imagine that she who was buried there was fair beyond her compeers. And it is true that she who lies under the green sod whence has sprung a wild rose-bush, self-sown, was to one loving heart one of the greatest and most marvellous beauties who ever lived; and who shall deny that she was, indeed, "Queen of Beauty and of Grace"?

JOY

Although it was December in the mountains, there came a day so strangely mild that it suggested spring. A strong, soft wind blew from the south, the sun's rays were distinctly warm, the snow around the trees melted imperceptibly until a curious effect was produced. It was as if a tree stood in a whirlpool of blue crystals. On the mountain road and on the cleared fields the tracks of wild animals and birds lost individual characteristics and ran together; the brook, which was almost a torrent in the spring, ran with an insistent roar, being augmented by soft droppings from the shaggy boughs which arched over it. The brook crossed the road under the bridge, within a few feet of William Doane's house. The house stood close to the road, after the old fashion of the times when men built as near the haunts of their kind as possible, when humans huddled together for protection against the savage and inhuman forces of matter and mind. The house was very old, and of an indescribable color, or, rather, lack of color. It was gloom rather than any tint on the old walls. The house looked almost, so black it was, as if it had been scorched by fire, and, in fact, the fierce suns and storms and winds of over a hundred years had burned it like fire. Still it was stanch. It had been built by an artisan who worked with the best of his strength. The roof did not sag, except for a slight depression around the central chimney. It was scaled with black shingles like some old sea monster, but it did not leak. William Doane cared for the old house as tenderly as if it had been some live thing. Not a black shingle flapped on the roof in a northern gale but the man was prompt in fastening it; not a leak when the wintry snow began to melt was neglected. The house, ancient as it was, would outlast the man, whose house of life had no such strenuous care for its earthly preservation. The walls sagged a little, the floors undulated like waves, the doors swung awry; that could not be avoided. It leaned, as the years went on, towards its final end, but it was no nearer falling than a stanch old tree whose roots held with a grasp of life to the soil, and even some rocks of the stern mountain-sides had a more precarious tenure of place than the old human dwelling.

And William Doane exercised the same zealous protection over all the simple, even primitive, furnishings which had endured from his mother's girlhood, and were, in fact, her marriage treasures. There was a wealth of old tables and dressers and bedsteads in the clean, icy rooms. William cleaned house, springs and autumns, as scrupulously as a woman. The old carpets sagged the line on the small level under the frown of the mountain back of the house every May and September. Every inch of woodwork was scrubbed. William purchased paint, and kept all the old wainscoting well whitened, the windows shone like sheets of emeralds from faithful polishing, the unused beds were even mounds of white linen, the house was a marvel of exquisite order and cleanliness, and all brought about by one man. He, however, lived only in two rooms of it, the kitchen and adjoining bedroom, except possibly in some summer days, when the heat was intense for a few hours even in that northern country. Then he would tiptoe carefully into the cool, dark sitting-room or the parlor, open a window a little way, and sit beside it with his book, gazing now and then at the familiar outlines of the opposite mountain and the long grandeur of the undulations with which it rose from his native valley.

The house, although a cottage, with the ceiling of the upper rooms slanting with the slant of the roof, was quite a large building, and had at one time, after the marriage of William Doane's parents, accommodated two families. The large kitchen and living-room had been divided and the great hearth cut in two. There were two square rooms, one on either side of the front door, and each family used one, and it was the same with the chambers. After the old people had gone, the son, William's father, used the whole house, but the kitchen partition remained. Indeed, each kitchen, although only half of the original, was a large room. It was the half with the southwest exposure which William tenanted, in his solitary estate. He had his nicely kept cooking-stove, his cushioned rocking-chair, his ancient table which served him for cooking and dining, and another old mahogany card-table, which he had removed from the parlor, for his books. That stood between the south windows, and the books were piled thereon in orderly fashion. William literally knew this small library by heart. For most of them he did not in one sense care, but they were to him like familiar companions of his solitude, to whom he owed a certain loyalty. He was conscious of being distinctly at variance with some of the views in these blackbound volumes of religious wisdom produced by the eminent theologians of the last century, and yet he got from them a certain keen enjoyment, they acting as stimulants upon his own mind, forcing him to silent but not the less eager controversy. Many an evening did William Doane engage in a spirited discussion with some long-dead divine, and come off glowing with triumph in the certainty of his own victory. There was about the man an innocent egotism which buoyed him up above the dead monotony of his life like wings. He had lived alone for fifteen years, ever since Grace Edwards had gone away, after his mother's death. Grace Edwards was the daughter of a farmer in Littlefield, twelve miles down country. She had come, when very young, not more than eighteen, to assist his mother in her household duties. She was practically homeless, her mother being dead and her father married to a woman who grudged her a home. So the girl, who was, moreover, delicate and young and small for her age, had been glad to enter into the dignified domestic service of that part of the country. William's mother had grown speedily very fond of the girl, had petted and coddled her, and come to think of her as her own, especially after Grace's father's death, leaving a will which gave everything to the step-mother and her children. William had been betrothed to her, after Grace had lived with himself and his mother three years, and was twenty years old. At that time the girl, although still delicate, was charming, small and gentle and fair, and yet with a quick flash of spirit in her blue eyes. William, who was grave and sedate as to demeanor, and of an awkward, shambling length of limb and neck, adored her. He worked the farm as it had never been worked before, for her sake. He made new ventures, he added by tiny driblets to his tiny income. He kept chickens and turkeys, and sold them, with vegetables, to a hotel about three miles distant. He in reality made an unusual income for a farmer in that part of the country. He purchased a parlor organ, and paid for Grace's music lessons in the village of Lowe, six miles away. He painted and furbished up the ancient vehicle in which he carried her back and forth for her lessons. Then he waited patiently during the hour and drove her home. Nothing could exceed the pride which filled him with a species of ecstasy as he sat by the girl's side, carefully driving his horse, which was somewhat skittish, and realized the eyes of people upon him and Grace, and was sure that they were coupling them in their thoughts and reflecting that this fair darling of a girl was his. Sometimes looking with a sort of shy reverence at the soft, fair face beside him, his own seemed to lose its characteristics and reflect hers as a mirror of love. At those times the man's face above the long, scrawny neck was a marvel, but the girl saw always the long neck and the awkwardness of her lover. She had agreed to marry him, but she did not like to look at him. She had a spiritual inclination towards this other faithful soul who loved her, but she also had a physical repulsion, which her soul was not strong enough to conquer. William about his strenuous work wore no collar, and there was something about the strangely humble and pathetic combination of long neck, prominent Adam's apple, no collar, and loving, patient, brown eyes which irritated her unaccountably. She could not always conceal it, although she tried. At last William's mother, who was a sharp woman, in spite of a premature feebleness, had taxed her with it. "I'd like to know why you act so standoffish with William," said she. Grace, who was timid, with a nature that swayed before a stronger one like a flower before a wind, had professed her innocence of any intentional coldness; still the older woman was not satisfied. She was constantly on the watch for some slight to her son, and at last matters reached a climax. It was one August evening, when William came home from the hay-field, where he had been gathering a small stock of rowen, that he heard, as he drew near the house, the sound of contending voices — his mother's, low-pitched almost as a man's, and the girl's, a sweet, strained treble. William was heated and dusty, his collarless neck looked longer than ever, every line and motion of his gaunt figure was awkward as he entered the sitting-room, which was the scene of contention. "You are a good-for-nothing, ungrateful girl," his mother said, distinctly, as he entered. She was pale and gasping for breath; she had a weak heart, but her voice was firm. Grace's face was flushed red with anger, her blue eyes had a hard glitter, her soft mouth was tense. She was transformed. "Then I will go away where my ingratitude will not trouble you any more," she declared, shrilly. Then the tears came. She felt blindly for her handkerchief, and could not find it, then put up both little hands before her face. William went soberly into his mother's bedroom, which opened out of the sitting-room, got a handkerchief, and gave it to the girl; then he spoke, looking from one to the other. "What is the matter?" he said.

His mother spoke first, to the accompaniment of the girl's sobs. "She treats you like a dog, and you haven't got sense enough to see it, nor spunk enough to pay her back," said she, fiercely.

"I have had no reason to find fault with Grace," William replied, with a certain dignity.

"Oh, stand up for her against your own mother if you want," his mother retorted. Then suddenly her face went paler, and she gasped frightfully, and William caught her and laid her on the lounge, while Grace, still sobbing, ran for water. William's mother only lived a week after that; the strain had been too much. After she was dead and buried, William and the girl had a discussion one evening. He had ventured to ask her to consent to an immediate marriage, but she refused. "I don't want to get married yet," said she, and remained firm with the impregnable firmness of a gentle nature when it is aroused.

"But, dear, how can we live on here unless we are," William said, finally, and at once his face and the girl's flushed scarlet.

"I'm going away," said she.

"Where?" asked William.

"I am going down to Littlefield."

"What will you do there? Go live with your step-mother?"

"I guess not. I am going to learn millinery. I am going into Mrs. Adkin's store. She said she would take me any time."

It was quite true that Grace had a pretty taste, and had trimmed her own hats with such success that the milliner's attention had been gained and the place offered.

William looked at her. "But there ain't any need of your working for a living," said he, pitifully. "I don't want you to work for a living, Grace."

"I want to be independent," said she.

"There is no need of your working for a living, even if you don't feel that you want to get married to me at all," William said, beseechingly. "You can live in one side of the house, and me in the other, Grace."

But the girl was firm in her determination. She packed her trunk, and William carried her in his light wagon to Littlefield, and left her at the milliner's. She was to board with her.

"Now any time you feel that you want to come back and live in the other side of the house you can," he said at parting. "You needn't worry about getting married if you don't want to. All I want is for you to be happy and not work too hard." There were tears in the man's eyes; the girl thanked him and said good-bye without looking at him. The milliner noticed at supper that Grace's eyes were red, and wondered if she had been crying.

As for William, he took up his lonely life with its compensations. He lived quite alone for fifteen years. He never heard from Grace, except indirectly. Shortly after her departure, the milliner with whom she worked moved to Boston and the girl with her. William grieved over it, and yet with a sort of sublimity of unselfishness, more for the girl's sake than his own, more because of the fear lest she be overworked, and not as well protected as he would have protected her. Still he knew that the milliner was a good woman, and he heard she was prospering, and Grace was still with her. Knowing this, and possessed by nature of almost abnormal optimism, his life was not unhappy. He seized upon all the small sweets, the minor alleviations of existence which came within his reach, and more than peace filled his soul. He was never idle, and his simple and primitive tasks were a keen delight to him. He kept his house in repair, he tended his grass lands and his garden, his chickens and his turkeys and his two Jersey cows, and in it all he took delight. The little front yard was gay with flowers every summer, and his very soul seemed to leap to new reaches of life and color to keep pace with the blossoms.

Then when the autumn came and the maples turned red and gold and the frost killed the flowers, his compensations were still enough to delight his soul. He banked his kitchen windows with potted plants. He laid in his winter store of firewood. He bought a few new books to read when he could not, on account of the impassable roads, go to Lowe to the library. He saw to it that his live-stock was housed warmly. He was happy even through the long winters. He was a happy man, in spite of the unfilled natural depths of his life. His great sweetness of nature had made even of the legitimate hunger of humanity a blessing for the promoting of spiritual growth. It had fostered within him that grand acquiescence which is the essence of perfect freedom. And his inner growth reacted upon his personal appearance. He dressed himself more carefully now, even alone as he was, with no human eye to see him for weeks at a time in winter. He bought collars and adjusted them carefully. He observed with a personal application the style of dress of the men at the hotel in the summer. He thought, with a sort of remorse, how seldom he had worn a collar when Grace had been at home. He saw his own awkward neck, his ungainly motions, and he held himself with a new dignity that overcame awkwardness. He had some clothes made in Lowe, instead of buying ready-made ones, as all his forebears had done. His first suit of clothes from the tailor gave him a certain awe, but he wore them as easily as a prince after the first. Marriageable women in Lowe began to notice him. He was invited in the winter to merrymakings there, but he never went. He was shy of other women than Grace from a species of uncalled-for loyalty, and never once had he given up her return some day. The hopefulness of his nature was inborn; he had not needed to cultivate it. For him storms had always been the precursors of sunshine; winds, of calm; spiritual cataclysms, of peace. He said always to himself during the long years that each brought Grace nearer. That some day, nearer by many, she would come. The love in his heart made of it a home and a nest, and sooner or later birds fly home. There was a pair of robins which returned to their nest in an old apple-tree on the south side of the house under the kitchen window every spring, and the sight always filled him with new certainty as to his own coming joy. Now it was December, and the tree was bare and the old nest plainly discernible. The snow had all dropped from the branches in the hot sun of that unusual December day, three days before Christmas. The branches looked black and dank, and every twig stood out silhouetted against the clear yellow of the sunset sky. In the sky at sunset was a low reef of violet cloud, which William eyed wisely. "It will be colder to-morrow," he told himself. When he returned from the barn, having finished his nightly tasks there, a blast from the northwest struck him. The thaw was over, and winter was again abroad. The man faced the bitter wind with delight. The thaw of the day, the soft droppings and gurglings, the warmth of the sun had awakened in him a happy sensitiveness; now the norther did the same. His soul gave out music in his ears to all the phases of nature. "It is cold again," he told himself, and he filled up his kitchen stove with wood, and got out the frying-pan to cook some ham and eggs for his supper, with a poetical rather than a physical sense of comfort and home in the midst of winter.

He sat at his neatly laid table, for he was as particular as a woman in such matters, and always had his napkin and white table-cloth and polished silver spoons, when suddenly he stopped eating and gave a great start. He had heard a noise on the other side of the partition which separated the kitchens. He sat motionless, listening, and as he listened his face became illuminated. He smiled, then he laughed silently, the laugh of delight of a child. He had not a doubt as to what the noise was. Grace had come home.

There was a door leading from one kitchen to the other. He rose and opened it, and there was the swift passing of a light and the rush of a figure from the other room. William stopped. Grace did not wish him to see her, and his mind fell at once into its attitude of acquiescence before a demand of love. But the cold air from the other kitchen was deadly. He did not shut the door, but hurriedly got some embers from his own glowing stove and carried them through on a shovel, and soon had a fire blazing in the other stove. He also carried in a slice of ham and some eggs and a plate of bread and butter and his own tea. He did it swiftly, for he knew that Grace must be shivering in one of the cold rooms the while. Then he returned to his own kitchen and closed the door and sat down before the fire and was happy. Soon he heard movements on the other side of the kitchen. He smelled the ham broiling. He finished his own supper with ineffable content. He never wondered how she had come. He was one to accept events as he did the weather — without question or investigation. She had come, and that was all he wished to know. All the concern he had was for her comfort. After a while he heard a door close on the other side, and he seized the opportunity to carry in a goodly store of wood for her stove. He also, with the thoughtfulness of a woman, took the sheets and quilts from the bed in the little room adjoining the kitchen, where she would presumably sleep for the warmth, and spread them on chairs before the stove, reasoning that Grace had always been sensitive to colds and inclined to be careless, and that it was dangerous to sleep in a long-unused bed. Then he retreated, after placing more ham and eggs and bread on the table, besides coffee and cream, for her breakfast.

The next morning he heard again the soft sounds on the other side of the partition; he smelled the coffee boiling. He killed a chicken that morning, dressed it, and roasted it with vegetables, and watched his chance to deposit it on the table in the other room. The day passed and he had not seen Grace, but he was not impatient. He told himself that for some reason she did not wish yet to see him, that he must wait and do what he could for her comfort. Suddenly it occurred to him it was only two days before Christmas, and a happy thought came to him. He would go to Lowe and buy some Christmas presents for Grace. That afternoon he put the horse in the old cutter and started. He was gone about two hours. It was a long drive over bad roads, and he was not an experienced shopper and somewhat hard to please. When he returned and had put the horse up and entered the kitchen with his arms full of parcels there was a loaf of frosted cake on the table. There was also a dish of cream toast set back on the stove to keep it warm, and the tea was steeping. The man laughed his silent laugh of extreme delight. He ate his supper, then examined his purchases. He had spent a good deal of money, more than he had ever spent in a day in his whole life, but he gloated over the presents without a thought of the cost. He had gotten more than the value of his money.

The weather was very bitter. He was careful to keep enough wood for the other kitchen stove in readiness; he was obliged to make frequent journeys, but he never saw Grace; she always fled before him. He was very patient, and none the less happy.

He remembered how once he and his mother had made a Christmas-tree for her, and her delight, and he resolved that she should have one now she had come home. So he took his axe, and went out into the woods and looked about for a perfect little tree.

He returned an hour later with a fine little tree, as symmetrical as a bouquet, and also with ground pine trailing over his shoulder. As he neared his old house a face swiftly disappeared from one of the front windows, and his own face lit up with a tender smile. That night, after he was sure that Grace had gone to bed, he set up the little fir-tree in the parlor on the other side of the house, hung the presents thereon, and laid some wood ready to kindle in the stove. Early the next morning he arose and lighted the fire in the parlor stove and made up his own kitchen fire and put the turkey in the oven. Then he returned to the parlor with more wood. The icy atmosphere had softened. The little tree made a brave show. He had hung some of the ground pine over two old steel engravings. It looked cheerful, although the morning was dark. There was a driving snow-storm. As he stood surveying the tree the door opened, and Grace entered, and he turned and they stood looking at each other. And the man saw that the woman had changed, that the face of the girl he had known was gone forever, that had he met her on the street of a strange city he might have passed her by unknowing; but the love in him leaped to meet the change, and he loved her as she stood there, timid, worn, and pale, as he had never loved her before.

"You have come," he said, and held out his hands to her, and she put her little, trembling, veinous ones in them.

"Yes," said she. Then she lifted her changed, thin little face to him, and spoke with a certain dignity. "I was not obliged to come," said she. "I have supported myself well. I have worked hard, but I have supported myself. I have money in the bank."

"You were always smart," said the man, gently, gazing at her with faithful eyes. Her own drooped before them.

"I never forgot you," said she, faintly, "and — and I heard you weren't married."

"Of course not," said the man. "You knew I was waiting for you, Grace." She made a little abrupt motion away from him at that. "If you want to we can live this way awhile, you in this side and me in the other," said the man, in a soothing voice, as if he were addressing a frightened child.

"The minister could not get here in such a storm as this," said she, and her averted face blazed. Then suddenly she turned, and her thin little arms were around his neck. "I'm willing to whenever you say so," she whispered. "I never ought to have gone."

"That is so," said William, "and you have had a hard time, dear; but, after all, if you had not gone there could not have been this coming back. You haven't looked at your Christmas-tree, Grace."

But she continued to look at him with childish blue eyes.

"Somehow you look different to me," she said.

"I have grown older," said William.

"No, you are handsome now," said she, and it was indeed a stately head of a man that she saw, and the thin, long neck with the prominent Adam's apple had filled out and was enclosed by a collar. Tears welled up in her blue eyes and her mouth quivered a little. She raised one little hand and touched her hair. "I have grown gray," said she, falteringly. "I don't look as I used." But the man smiled down at her, and suddenly she saw herself as she was in his heart, and a look of wonder and rapture came over her face, transfiguring it, for in a second, as it were, she mastered the conception of love. "I am sorry I went away," she said, "and I will try to make up for it."

William laughed. "Look at your tree, dear," he said.

"I have hung a present on it for you, too," said she.

That night the storm cleared away. It was arranged that the next morning they were to drive down to Lowe and be married. After all was still in Grace's side of the house, William sat at a window in his kitchen gazing out at the sky in which the stars blazed with a wonderful nearness and surprise of reality. He thought of the sleeping woman on the other side who was to be his wife with a tenderness which was akin to pain, and then a solitariness of joy was over him.

THE REIGN
OF THE DOLL

There was a great storm. Fidelia Nutting was too frightened and excited to go to bed. It was eleven o'clock; three hours before, at eight o'clock, she had opened the door into her bedroom in order that the warmth of the sitting-room should temper the freezing atmosphere before she retired. She sat where she could see the peaceful white slope of the feather-bed; her head was heavy with sleep, but the strain of her nerves kept her awake. Fidelia was exceedingly timid, and even overawed, by any unusual stress of nature. Summer thunder-storms had always rendered her for the time a mild maniac, winds seemed to penetrate her soul, winter snows to enter and sift into the farthest crannies of her thoughts. This storm was sleet rather than snow. The wind raged. It seemed to pounce upon the house and shake it like a wild beast, then retreat, muttering, to some awful lair of storm, to return with a new gathering of fury.

Fidelia cowered and shivered, with a roll of fearful eyes. She was a large, elderly woman with the soul of a child. She was entirely alone in her little house; over across the street, in the large, old mansion-house of the Nuttings, her sister Diantha was also alone. Now and then Fidelia went to her window, that looked across the street, and saw with a thrill of half resentful comfort her sister Diantha's light. She reflected that Diantha also had always been afraid in a storm, though not as afraid as she — or not owning to it.

"She always used to keep her lamp burning when there was a thunder-storm and when the wind was high," reflected Fidelia. Diantha's lamp was set on a table in the centre of her sitting-room, in a direct line with Fidelia's window. A great beam of yellow light shone through the window — through the shreds of snow which clung like wool to the sashes, through the icy veil of sleet, through the foliage of the geraniums in Fidelia's beautiful window garden. Fidelia was a little afraid that the cold wind might injure her flowers, but she would not lower her curtain, because she was shamefacedly desirous of the company of Diantha's light.

Suddenly she heard a gathering flurry of sleigh-bells. They increased until they seemed in the room; then they stopped suddenly. Fidelia's heart leaped for fear.

"Something has stopped here," she gasped. It was unprecedented for anything to stop there at that hour and in such a storm.

She shaded her eyes, and peered fearfully and cautiously from the window around her geraniums. She could see a dark shape at the opposite window, blotting out the lamplight, and she knew that Diantha was also looking. A man's figure, gigantic in a fur coat, lumbered slantingly through the drifts of the path to the front door. Fidelia put a little worsted shawl over her head, took her lamp, and crept tremblingly through the freezing front entry in response to the knock. Her bell was out of order.

"Who's there?" she asked.

"Express!" he shouted, in an angry voice, and Fidelia turned the key and opened the door. The fur of the expressman's coat stood out, stiffly pointed with ice; his cap looked like an ice helmet. "Express, ma'am," he said, in a hoarse voice, and the package was in Fidelia's hand and he was gone. Then the wind came in a wild gust, and Fidelia fled before it with her streaming lamp. Back in the warm sitting-room she set the lamp safely on the table; then she stood gazing at her package. It was a long box, very nicely wrapped in thick paper and securely tied. Fidelia did not connect it with Christmas; Christmas presents were not within her present environments. She examined the package carefully, and saw that the address was correct — Miss Fidelia Nutting, North Abbot, and it was marked paid, with a blue pencil. She laid the package on the table, and seated herself near it in her rocking-chair. Another gust of wind came, and the bombardment of the sleet upon the window was frightful; it seemed as if the panes must be shattered. She looked at the package on the table, and a curious fear of it came over her. The unwontedness of that and the unwontedness of the storm seemed one, and instinct with terror.

"I'd like to know what's in that bundle," she whispered, with fearful eyes on it. She got up and gazed across the street at her sister's lamp, which still shone to comfort her. The dark figure, however, moved before it in a second. "She's looking out," she thought, with that curious mixture of timidity and anger and affection with which she always thought of her sister. She and Diantha had quarrelled over the distribution of the property after their mother died. Diantha had taken the old homestead and less money, and gone to live there alone. Fidelia had taken more money and the small cottage, and gone to live there. They spoke sternly when they met; they never exchanged visits; there was between them a sort of dignified hostility, to which they did not own. Although all the village knew that there was enmity between the sisters, none knew which of the two originated it, which had demanded the peculiar arrangement of property and the living part. Fidelia felt a certain sympathy with Diantha because of the express package. She knew how curious Diantha was, though she would not own to it. Curiosity at its extreme is like unslaked thirst. "Poor Diantha, she's just dying to know what is in that bundle," she said to herself. She, aside from her vague alarm over it, was loath to open it in the face of this eager, unsatisfied curiosity over the way. She watched her sister's light opposite. She had a desperate hope that she would keep it burning all night; but about half-past ten it went suddenly out. "Oh, dear," groaned Fidelia. Loneliness went over her like a deep sea. New terror of the package seized her. She felt that nobody would send it to her with any good purpose. Her nervous terror had fairly for the time being unsettled her reason. Then she heard someone at the door. She waited, hoping that she might be mistaken, that it was the wind. But it came again. There was a sharp pounding on the door panels; it was impossible to think it was anything else.

Fidelia pulled her little shawl closely over her head, took up her lamp, and went forth into the cold front entry. The pounding came on the door with redoubled impetus. The caller had seen the lamp through the side-lights.

"Who is it?" cried Fidelia, in a voice which rang strange to her own ears. She was almost in convulsions of terror.

"Diantha," responded a shrill voice from outside. "Let me in quick; it's a terrible storm."

Then Fidelia set her lamp on the entry table, and fumbled in a tumult of surprise and delight with the bolt and the key and a chain. As the door opened, the lamp blazed high and went out. Diantha and Fidelia rushed upon the door, and together forced it back and locked it.

"Come into the sitting-room, Diantha," said Fidelia, in a trembling voice. "Look out you don't run into anything; it's very dark." Fidelia felt timidly for her sister's hand, and led her, feeling her way carefully, into the sitting-room.

Fidelia got a match and fumbled her way back to the entry, got the lamp and lighted it, and put it in its usual place on the sitting-room table. Then the sisters looked at each other. Each looked curiously shamefaced. Diantha was smaller than Fidelia, but more incisive. She was rather pretty, with a sharply cut, cameo-like face framed in white hair, which was now indecorously tossed about her temples. She began smoothing it impatiently.

"I never saw a worse night," said she.

"It's a terrible storm," assented Fidelia. It was pleasant to find a common grievance. "Do you want a brush and comb?" asked she.

"Yes, I guess I'd better smooth my hair a little," said Diantha; and Fidelia got her brush and comb from the bedroom. She watched her sister standing before the sitting-room mirror, which hung between the front windows, and her whole face was changed. Whatever bitterness had been in her heart towards Diantha was lost sight of in her joy over companionship in this night of storm.

"It's a dreadful storm," said she.

"Yes, it is, "assented Diantha. "I could hardly get over here. The telephone-wire is down, and the branches are crashing off the trees. There's a big maple branch right 'side of your front gate. I had to step over the end of it. It's awful."

"It's worse than it was," said Fidelia.

"Yes, it's worse than it was when the expressman came." Diantha looked hard at the package on the table.

Fidelia was slow to wrath, but all at once she had an impulse of indignation. So that was all her sister had come over there for — just curiosity to see what was in that package, when she knew how frightened she was in a storm, how frightened she had always been. She sat down in the rocking-chair, and her large face took on an expression at once sulky and obstinate.

"Yes," she said, dryly, "I guess it is worse than it was when the expressman came." Then she said no more. She rocked slowly back and forth; a fierce rattle of sleet came on the window-panes. Diantha carried the brush and comb back to the bedroom; her white hair shone like silver; then she returned, and stood looking out at the black night pierced by the whiteness of the storm.

"Don't you feel afraid that your geraniums will get frozen, quite so close to the window?" she asked. "That Lady Washington lays right against the pane, and it is so cold that the window is frosting, beside the sleet."

Fidelia softened a little. "Maybe there is some danger," she said.

"Suppose we move them back a little?" said Diantha. "We can move them together, I guess."

Fidelia rose, and she and Diantha took hold of the flower-stand and moved it slightly away from the window.

"I guess that is safer," said Diantha. She looked at the package on the table again, but Fidelia was rocking back and forth with the old look of obstinacy on her face. Diantha also sat down near the stove. A great gust of wind shook the house; a tree crashed somewhere.

"It is an awful storm," remarked Diantha.

Fidelia felt such a thrill of thankfulness for companionship in the midst of that terrible attack of wind that she melted. "Yes," she said, "it is awful."

"It makes me think of stories I used to read of folks in a fort being besieged by Indians," said Diantha, looking at the package.

Fidelia's eyes followed hers. "Yes," she said, "it does."

"I suppose you don't want to go to bed yet?" said Diantha, rather formally. "I am not keeping you up?"

"No," said Fidelia.

"I thought you didn't use to go to bed in a hard storm," said Diantha, "and I felt kind of nervous alone, and I saw your light burning."

Fidelia's face lightened. So Diantha had not come over wholly for the sake of curiosity. Fidelia felt pleased to think her sister had felt the need of her, even selfishly. Her eyes and Diantha's both fell upon the package at the same time; then they met.

"I haven't opened it yet," said Fidelia, quite easily. She laughed.

Diantha laughed too. "You don't seem to be in much of a hurry to see your Christmas present," said she.

"Oh, I don't believe it can be a Christmas present."

"It must be."

"Who could have sent me one?"

"I don't know, but somebody must have."

"Perhaps I had better see what it is," said Fidelia. She rose, and Diantha hesitated a second; then she rose, and both women stood over the package on the table. Fidelia began carefully untying the string.

"Why don't you cut it?" asked Diantha.

"It's a very nice string," replied Fidelia, who was thrifty. Her thrift had made some of the difference between herself and her sister.

She strove hard with the knot, which was difficult. Diantha pushed her away, and untied it herself with firm, nervous fingers. Then she flung the string to her sister.

"Here's your string," said she, but with entire good-nature. She even laughed indulgently. Fidelia then wound the string carefully, while Diantha lifted the lid from the box. Both women gave little gasps of astonishment.

"Goodness!" cried Diantha. "Who ever could have?"

"I don't know," responded Fidelia, feebly. They both stared a second at each other, then again at the box. In the box, in a nest of tissue-paper, lay a large doll. The doll's eyes were closed, but she smiled in her doll-sleep — a smile of everlasting amiability and peace. Golden ringlets clustered around her pink-and-white countenance, her little kid arms and hands lay supine at her side, her little kid toes stuck up meekly side by side. The doll was entirely undressed, except for a very brief under-garment of coarse muslin.

"It's a doll," gasped Diantha.

"Yes, Diantha," gasped Fidelia.

"Who could have sent you a doll?" inquired Diantha, with some sternness.

"I don't know," replied Fidelia.

"There must be some mistake," said Diantha.

Fidelia's face, which had worn an expression of secret delight, fell. "I suppose so," she said.

Both women stared at the doll, as if under a species of fascination. The storm roared harder, the sleet beat against the window as if it would break the glass, another tree branch crashed, but they did not heed it. They continued to stare at the doll.

"She isn't dressed," said Fidelia, finally, with a tender cadence in her voice.

"No, she isn't," returned Diantha.

Diantha then lifted the doll very carefully and delicately by the middle of its small back. The doll's eyes immediately flew open, and seemed to survey them with intelligent and unswerving joy.

"Her eyes open and shut," remarked Diantha. She then pressed the small body a little harder, and there came a tiny, squeaking cry. "It cries," proclaimed Diantha.

Fidelia simply stared.

Diantha looked speculative. "Most probably this doll belongs to the little Merrill girl that lives next door," said she.

"Perhaps it does," replied Fidelia.

"I guess you had better take it over there to-morrow morning and ask her mother."

"I suppose I had."

Diantha and Fidelia sat down after Diantha had placed the doll carefully back in the box, but she did not replace the lid. The two women rocked, and listened to the storm, which seemed to increase.

"There's no going to bed to-night, I suppose," said Diantha, with an angry inflection. She scowled at the storm beating at the windows.

The two rocked awhile longer. It was past midnight.

"That doll makes me think of that one I had when I was a child," said Diantha, in a tone of indignant reminiscence.

"It looks a good deal like mine, too," said Fidelia, in a softer tone.

"It seems," said Diantha, still in an indignant tone, "a pity to give away a doll to any child, not dressed."

Fidelia, looking at Diantha, blushed all over her delicate old face, and Diantha also blushed.

"Yes, it does," said Fidelia, in a hesitating voice.

"It's a shame," said Diantha.

"Yes," said Fidelia — "yes, I think it is a shame."

"I suppose you have a lot of pieces in the house?" said Diantha. She did not look at Fidelia then; she gazed out of the window. "It is a dreadful storm," she murmured, before Fidelia had a chance to reply, as if her mind were really not upon the doll at all.

"Yes, I have," replied Fidelia, with subdued eagerness.

"Well, I suppose the little Merrill girl would think a lot more of the doll if it was dressed; it would be a shame to give her one that wasn't, and if we've got to sit up for the storm we may as well do something. It wasn't ever my way to sit idle."

"I know it wasn't, sister," agreed Fidelia, falling insensibly into her old manner of addressing Diantha. "I've got a great many real pretty pieces," she said.

"Handy?"

"They are up-garret."

"Well, what if they are? I ain't afraid to go up-garret for them. You'd better light the lantern, that's all. I don't think we'd better carry a lamp up there; the wind blows too hard."

"I'll get it right away," said Fidelia, fairly tremulous with excitement.

"Have you got any pieces of that blue silk dress you had when you were nineteen years old?"

"Yes, I have some nice pieces."

"My green silk would make something handsome, but the pieces of that are all over at my house."

"I've got a big piece of that," said Fidelia. "You gave me some for patchwork years ago, and I did not begin to use it up; and I've got some of that pink satin I had when Abigail Upham was married; and I've got some dotted muslin, and some of that spriggled muslin, and plenty of old linen, and some narrow lace, and some ribbon."

"You'd better get the lantern, and we'll get the pieces and go right to work," said Diantha, rising with alacrity.

The two women went forthwith to the garret, stepping cautiously over the loose flooring, and peering timorously into the recumbent shadows beneath the eaves by the flashing light of the lantern which Fidelia carried. The pieces were in two old trunks and a blue cotton bag. They collected a quantity of remnants of silk and satin and linen, and went back down-stairs to the sitting-room. Fidelia was trembling with the cold.

"You'd better sit close to the stove, or you'll catch your death," said Diantha, and she looked kindly at her sister.

"Yes, I will," replied Fidelia, gratefully.

"I'll set the lamp on the stand, and then you can see," said Diantha.

The two sisters, seated close to the warm stove, with the stand between them, went to work with half-shamed delight. They cut and made the tiny garments for the smiling doll, while the storm raged outside. They paid very little attention to it. They were absorbed.

"Suppose we make the pink satin just the way yours was made," suggested Diantha.

"With a crosswise flounce," said Fidelia, happily.

"And a little lace spencer cape."

"My old doll had one," said Fidelia.

"And so did mine."

"All our dolls used to dress alike."

"Yes, I know they did."

"We used to take a sight of comfort playing with them, sister."

"Yes, we did," agreed Diantha, harshly, "but those days are over."

Fidelia felt a little rebuked. "Yes, I know they are," she replied, meekly.

"We might make a dress of dotted muslin over the blue silk, like those our dolls used to have," said Diantha, in a softer voice.

"Yes, we might," Fidelia said, delighted.

As the two women worked, their faces seemed to change. They were tall and bent, with a rigorous bend of muscles not apparently so much from the feebleness and relaxing of age as from defiance to the stresses of life; both sisters' backs had the effect of stern walkers before fierce winds; their hair was sparse and faded, brushed back from thin temples, with nothing of the grace of childhood, and yet there was something of the immortal child in each as she bent over her doll-clothes. The contour of childhood was evident in their gaunt faces, which suddenly appeared like transparent masks of age; the light of childhood sparkled in their eyes; when they chattered and laughed one would have sworn there were children in the room. And, strangest of all, their rancor and difference seemed to have vanished; they were in the most perfect accord.

They worked all night, until the triumphant pallor of dawn overcame the darkness and the window-panes were outlined in blue through the white shades. It cleared just before daylight.

"I declare, it's morning," said Diantha.

"We've worked all night," said Fidelia, in an awed tone.

"Better work than sit still," said Diantha. "You'd better put the lamp out."

Fidelia put out the lamp and pulled up a window-curtain.

"The storm is over," said she, "but it is awful! Just look, sister."

Diantha and Fidelia stood at the window and surveyed the ruin outside. The yard and the road were strewn with the branches of the trees; the trees, lopped and mutilated, stood cased in a glittering white mail over their lost members. It was a sylvan battlefield, where the victors had barely come off with their lives.

"It's dreadful; you can't get home yet a while," said Fidelia.

"I guess I can manage," said Diantha, suspiciously. She wondered if Fidelia wanted to be rid of her.

But Fidelia was looking at her with the expression of a child who wants to make up. "I thought I'd make some of those light biscuits you used to like for breakfast," said she.

"I don't see as I can get home before breakfast," said Diantha. Then she added, in another voice, "Yes, I always did like those light biscuits, sister."

"I've got some honey, too," said Fidelia.

"If there is anything I do like it is light biscuit and honey," said Diantha.

"We can finish dressing the doll after breakfast," ventured Fidelia, radiantly.

"Yes, we can. It's a shame to give a child a doll that ain't dressed."

The sisters worked until late afternoon on the doll's small wardrobe. Everything was complete, from the tiny stockings and slippers to the hat of drawn pink silk, after the style of one which Diantha's doll had owned a half-century before. When at last the doll was arrayed in her pink silk frock, her lace spencer cape, her pink hat trimmed with a fall of lace, under which her rosy face with its unswerving smile looked at her benefactors, they were radiant.

"I call that a very beautiful doll, sister," said Fidelia.

"She certainly is," agreed Diantha.

Fidelia looked at Diantha, and Diantha returned the look. A sudden cloud was over both faces.

"I suppose," said Fidelia, slowly, "we had better —"

"Yes, I suppose so," said Diantha, harshly.

"Before it gets any later," said Fidelia, with a sigh.

"Yes, I suppose so."

"To-morrow is Christmas. Maybe her mother wants to hang it on the tree."

"Very likely."

"Well, will you take it over, or will I?"

"I had just as lief."

"I will if you don't feel like it."

Still neither offered to move. Both regarded the doll, then again each other.

"That Merrill child is not nearly old enough to have a doll like that," said Diantha, suddenly.

"I don't think she is either," said Fidelia.

"No, she is not. It is strange people will buy such dolls for children who are no older."

"Especially since she has such handsome clothes."

"She would spoil the clothes in no time."

"Yes; she would let her wear that pink silk and her best hat every day."

"That little Merrill girl is not old enough to take care of that doll," said Diantha, with emphasis, and with much the same tone as if she had spoken of a baby. She gathered up the doll with determination.

Fidelia sighed. "Are you going to take her over there now?" said she. It was noticeable that both sisters now spoke of the doll as she and her.

"No, I am not. I am going to take her home," declared Diantha.

"You are not going to take her over to the Merrills, sister?"

"No, I am not. That child is not old enough."

Fidelia looked scared, and also aggrieved. "But," she said, "that doll was left here; I don't think you have any right to take her away, Diantha. If either of us is going to keep her, it ought to be the one to whom it was sent."

Diantha surveyed her sister with an injured expression. "Fidelia Nutting," said she, "you don't think — you don't really think — I would do such a thing as that? Of course I wasn't going to take the doll away from you, although she does not really belong to either of us. Of course I know that you have the first claim. I was just going to take her to my house for a while, and I thought you would come over and have tea with me. I have some of that damson sauce you like, and the pound-cake and a mince-pie, and I will make some of those griddle-cakes with butter and sugar and nutmeg on them. It's lonesome for you here alone, with the roads not cleared enough so anybody can get in very easy, and it's lonesome for me. I thought maybe you'd come over, but if — you don't want to —"

"Oh, sister, I shall be very happy to come over, and I haven't had any of those griddle-cakes since mother died. I never got the knack of making them myself. I'll get my shawl and hood."

"You'd better wrap up warm," said Diantha; "it's cleared off cold by the looks. And you'd better fix your fire so you can leave it. Maybe you'll feel as if you could stay all night."

When the two sisters crossed the road together, stepping among the débris of the storm, which had not yet been fully cleared away, the neighbors within range stared. In the Merrill house, next to Fidelia's, the width of a wide yard distant, three faces were in the sitting-room window — Mrs. Merrill's, her unmarried sister's, and little Abby Merrill's, round and rosy, flattened against the glass.

"Did you ever!" cried Annie Bennett, Mrs. Merrill's sister. "There go the Nuttings across the street together. I wonder if they have made up."

"They are going into Diantha's house," said Mrs. Merrill, with wonder. "I wonder if they have made up. I don't believe one has been into the other's house since their mother's funeral."

"Maybe they have," said Annie Bennett.

"Mamma," said little Abby Merrill, "what do you spect Miss Nutting is carrying under her shawl?"

"I don't know, dear," said Mrs. Merrill.

"It looks like a dolly," said little Abby Merrill, wisely.

Mrs. Merrill and Annie Bennett laughed. "I guess Miss Diantha Nutting isn't going around carrying dollies," said Mrs. Merrill. "I guess you must be mistaken, darling."

Annie Bennett could scarcely stop laughing at the idea of Diantha Nutting carrying about a doll. But she suddenly remembered something. "Why, there's that parcel that came here for Fidelia by mistake last night," she said, chokingly. "Seeing her carry a parcel makes me remember that. I had quite forgotten it.

She ought to have it, I suppose. Perhaps it is a Christmas present."

"Yes, she ought to have it," said Mrs. Merrill, turning away from the window as the door of the opposite house closed after Diantha's and Fidelia's shawled and hooded figures.

"I'll run over there and carry it," said Annie Bennett.

But little Abby interposed. She was wild to get out-of-doors after her imprisonment by the storm, and she was wild to carry a Christmas present. "Oh, mamma, let me carry it," she begged.

Her mother looked doubtful. "I don't know whether you can get over all those tree-branches without falling and hurting yourself, darling," she said.

"Oh yes, I can," pleaded little Abby.

"I don't believe it will hurt her any if she wants to go," said her aunt, Annie Bennett.

So little Abby Merrill, carefully wrapped against the cold, went across the street, picking her way among the fallen branches, with her mother watching anxiously, and carried the parcel to Diantha Nutting's door. "My mamma sent me over wif zis," said she — for Abby could not say "th" — "My mamma sent me over wif zis, zat was left at our house by a spressman by mistake last night." Little Abby Merrill never knew why Miss Diantha Nutting's face looked suddenly very strange to her, but she felt vaguely alarmed, and shrank back when Diantha spoke.

"Thank you, child," said she, in rather a deep voice, and she took the parcel.

Miss Fidelia Nutting's face was visible behind her sister's, and it wore a similar expression. "Oh, sister!" she gasped when little Abby Merrill had gone trotting, stepping high in her little red leggings, across the street. She was a stout little girl, and planted her little feet in a sturdy fashion. "Oh, sister!"

Diantha clutched her hard. "Come into the house," said she.

The two returned to the warm sitting-room, and then they looked at each other like two confederates in crime.

"Oh, sister, it is dreadful!" said Fidelia, faintly. "That doll must belong to little Abby Merrill, and this bundle she brought must be a Christmas present that somebody has sent me, and somehow the expressman made a mistake. She ought to have her, sister."

"Well," said Diantha, "go over there and carry her if you want to, then."

Fidelia hung her head. "She is a pretty small child to have such a doll, I suppose," she faltered.

"Then don't talk about it," said Diantha. "Why don't you

open your parcel?"

Fidelia opened the parcel; inside the brown wrapping-paper was a nice white one tied with lavender ribbon. She untied the dainty bows, and unfolded a fleecy white shawl.

"Who gave it to you?" said Diantha.

Fidelia looked at the slip of paper pinned to a corner of the shawl. On it was written, "With Xmas greetings from Salome H. May."

"It's Salome May," she said.

"She always makes a sight of Christmas," said Diantha.

"I suppose she sent it because I gave her old-fashioned pinks out of my garden last summer," said Fidelia.

"It's a pretty shawl," said Diantha, with no enthusiasm.

"Yes, it is," said Fidelia; "but I never was in the habit of wearing a knit shawl in the house much." She laid the shawl on the table. "I suppose she sent the doll to the little Merrill girl," she added, after a pause.

"Very likely. She and Annie Bennett are intimate."

"Diantha, don't you suppose we are doing a dreadful thing?"

"No, I don't. I don't see why we are. We are not stealing that doll, are we?"

"No-o, I don't suppose we are stealing her," said Fidelia, hesitatingly.

"I am not stealing her, anyway. My conscience is clear. All I am doing is keeping her a little while, until the little Merrill girl is old enough to play with her and not destroy her."

"Oh, of course, that is all I am doing, too, sister."

Diantha Nutting prepared tea in the old dining-room, and she set the table with her mother's old blue Canton china and the best silver teapot and cream-pitcher. There were the griddle-cakes piled in a golden mound sprinkled with sugar and nutmeg; there was the damson sauce; there the pound-cake; but neither sister could eat much. The doll in her brave attire lay on the sitting-room table beside the shawl. Both felt, though they would not confess it to each other or herself, like greedy and dishonest children stealing another child's doll on Christmas-eve. But they were yet firm. Fidelia remained with Diantha that night, and Fidelia occupied her old room out of Diantha's. Neither slept much. Often one called to the other in the darkness of the night: "Fidelia, are you asleep?" "Diantha, are you asleep?" Both were thinking of the doll and the little Merrill girl, and their consciences, which were their New England birthrights, never slumbered nor slept.

The next morning at breakfast — which they did not care for, although it was as desirable as the tea of the night before, being composed of hot biscuits and honey, and ham and eggs and coffee — they looked at each other.

"Sister, I can't do it. I can't keep it up any longer," said Fidelia, suddenly and piteously.

"Well, I suppose she'll have to have her, if she does destroy her," said Diantha, grimly. Then she took another biscuit.

"I guess I'll have another biscuit too," said Fidelia.

After breakfast Fidelia crossed the road to the Merrill house. She rang the bell, trembling, and Annie Bennett came to the door.

"Here is a doll," said Fidelia, trembling. She extended the doll in her pink silk hat and her spencer cape. "Here is a doll that was left at my house by mistake. My name was on the paper, but I guess she made a mistake on account of sending so many presents. Salome H. May sent me a shawl, and I guess she must have meant the doll for little Abby."

But Annie Bennett stared wonderingly at the doll. "Why, no," said she. "Salome sent a doll for Abby two days ago. She can't have sent this to Abby. Abby has five dolls this Christmas, anyway. It can't be Abby's. I don't know of any one else who could have sent her a doll. Was your name on the wrapper?"

"Yes, it was," admitted Fidelia, a great shamefaced hope in her heart.

Annie Bennett laughed. "Well," she said, "as near as I can find out, the doll is yours, Miss Fidelia. I guess somebody thought you and your sister needed a doll to play with."

Fidelia was aware of the friendly sarcasm, but quite unmoved by it. She blushed, but she smiled happily. "It is queer who could have sent it," said she, "but I guess it can't belong to little Abby."

"No, I know it can't," said Annie Bennett.

Annie Bennett and Mrs. Merrill and little Abby Merrill, with her new doll from Salome H. May in her arms, all watched Fidelia Nutting cross the street to Diantha's.

"She skips along like a child," said Mrs. Merrill.

"She is a good deal spryer than Abby," laughed Annie Bennett. "You ought to have seen how that doll was dressed; the funniest old-fashioned things. I wonder if she and Miss Diantha dressed it. I didn't know but she would leave it for Abby anyhow."

"I suppose they will give it to some child," said Mrs. Merrill. "I suppose she thought Abby had dolls enough. I'd like to know who sent her that doll."

"I know what I think," said Annie Bennett. "I think Salome May had a doll left over, and sent it to Fidelia Nutting for a joke.

It's just like her."

"Maybe she did," said Mrs. Merrill, laughing.

But Fidelia and Diantha themselves were the children who loved the doll, and they could not spare her to another child. When Fidelia ran into the sitting-room of her sister's house with the doll in her arms, Diantha stared.

"What have you brought her back for?" she asked, shortly.

"Oh, sister, the little Merrill girl has a doll from Salome H. May. This isn't her doll. It must have been sent to me."

"Fidelia Nutting, who do you suppose did such a silly thing as to send a doll to you?"

"I don't know, sister."

"Well," said Diantha, "There's one thing certain: if we don't know whom she belongs to, there's nothing to do but to keep her. If she wasn't meant for you, it's the fault of the sender."

"Maybe we shall find out sometime about her," said Fidelia. But they never did.

"Well, you had better stay to dinner," said Diantha. "I hailed the butcher and got a chicken, and I've got pudding on boiling."

When the two sat at dinner, casting stray glances at the doll on the sitting-room table, Diantha spoke.

"Look here, Fidelia," said she. "I've been thinking. Suppose you rent that house you live in, and come and live with me. Nobody knows how much longer we've got to live, anyhow, and we can put our means together and have a girl to wait on us; we ain't either of us fit to live alone, and I guess we can get along. We used to get along well enough when we were children."

"Yes, we did," said Fidelia, cheerfully. "I'll come if you want me to, sister."

In the afternoon the sisters sat together in the sitting-room of the Nutting house. They were making some more clothes for a doll — a lavender silk frock from an old one of Diantha's, and a little black silk mantilla. They sat close to the window to catch the waning wintry sunlight — two old sisters, come together after years of estrangement, through the mediation of the universal play-thing of childhood, which had come to them out of a mystery, into a common ground of old love and memories.

"I suppose we ought to name this doll," said Diantha. "We always did name our dolls."

"Yes, I guess we had better name it," agreed Fidelia.

"We will keep her for little girls to play with if any happen in with their mothers," said Diantha. "And if a child asks what her name is, we ought to have something to say."

"Yes, I think so."

"Well?" said Diantha, interrogatively.

Fidelia blushed redly before her own sentiment; then she spoke. "I guess Peace would be a good name," said she, with a soft little shamed laugh at her sister.

"Well," said Diantha.

The two sisters continued sewing on the doll's clothes while the light lasted, their heads bent close together with loving accord, and the doll was between them, smiling with inscrutable inanity.

THE CHANCE
OF ARAMINTA

"I'm ready for another basket, sister!" cried Araminta.

For the last six months, and more or less through the whole year since the preceding Christmas, Araminta and Sarah White had been preparing presents for the neighborhood and all their relatives. It was the day before Christmas now, and Araminta was distributing them, as was her annual wont. She was wrapped up warmly — it was very cold — and she carried a large empty basket. "Here, fill it up again, quick!" she cried, and pulled off her shawl to help, herself. Araminta's older sister Sarah and the visiting cousin, Mrs. Martha Spear from Ohio, began gathering up small, neat parcels in white paper, tied with red cord, from the table and sofa where they were piled.

"Land! what a lot of folks you do remember!" said the cousin, placing parcels gingerly in the basket.

"We don't leave out a single soul for half a mile each way," said Sarah, proudly, "or, rather, Araminta don't. She does the most of it."

"I don't do any more than you do, sister," said Araminta. "I tell you those Lumkins children were tickled when they saw me coming, poor little things. Every head was in the window, noses flat as dabs of putty against the glasses, the whole six."

"Six children?" said the cousin.

"Yes, six," replied Sarah, "and the father no money, and the mother no strength, all six sickly."

"And dirty," added Araminta, happily.

"Dreadful!" said the cousin.

"I can't help feelin' so sometimes," agreed Sarah, who was at times gently pessimistic.

But Araminta laughed with confidence. "Nonsense!" said she, placing another parcel. "You ought to have seen them just now. It is six times as much fun Christmas as one child could have, and who's going to say it isn't worth while? And I guess there's fun enough left over from this Christmas for their whole lives. You'd ought to have seen them, how they tickled and laughed, sickly, and dirty, and everything. Mother used to say she didn't want to have a cat put out of the world that took a mite of comfort in it, and I guess six children as happy as those this morning are more than cats. Their mother was pleased, too."

"Araminta made a nice flannel wrapper for her — cut and

made it herself," said Sarah.

"She put it right on to see how it fitted, and she looked as pretty as a picture in it," said Araminta. The basket was full again, and she replaced the shawl over her shoulders and pinned it tightly around her neck. She gathered up the basket on her arm, and stood in the doorway a second, smiling at the two women before starting.

"Jest look at her!" cried the cousin, with a mixture of admiration and wonder and amusement. "If she ain't the happiest-looking mortal I ever laid eyes on."

Indeed, Araminta White, middle-aged, single, with the faded dulness of advancing life on her thin face, with sparse gray hair, merely a line showing under her hood above a lift of candid forehead, which was heavily lined, seemed to give out a glow of pure delight. She was wonderful. Her blue eyes shone with something better than the youth of the flesh. She smiled a smile which took hold of immortal bliss. She looked like an incarnate joy, and the women dimly sensed it. Then she turned and went out, laughing happily like a child, like a goddess who holds youth and childhood forever. "I am happy," she called back. "My looks don't belie me! Nobody knows how I look forward to this all the year!"

"She gives right through the year, too," Sarah said, when the door had shut and Araminta had passed the windows. "I never saw anybody take so much comfort giving presents as Araminta. She can't give much in one way, either, for we haven't money enough, but she's a wonderful manager. She don't stint at home for any comforts, and we both have enough to look respectable."

"You both look real nice," said the cousin.

"But somehow she manages to get enough to give away. She makes her clothes hang on to beat everything, and she fixes them over and over. That coat she wears she's had ten years. I told her she ought to have a new one this winter, but she took the money and divided it, and bought two little jackets for the Monroe girls, and I wish you could see Araminta's face when she sees those two girls going by in those jackets. If she saw herself as beautiful as an angel and dressed like a queen, in a looking-glass, she couldn't look any more pleased."

The cousin sat swaying back and forth in the rocking-chair. She had not seen these relatives for years — not since her own girlhood, when she lived in the same village. Now her husband was dead, and she had returned middle-aged, stout, and rather opulent, to take up some of the old threads of her life. She had arrived the day before, and was to spend a number of weeks with Sarah and Araminta. "Araminta ain't changed very much in her looks," said she, finally, with a reminiscent expression.

"No," replied Sarah, "I don't see as she has. Of course living with anybody right along, it's harder to tell." Sarah was perhaps ten years older than the visiting cousin, tall and slender, with an ineffaceable dignity of mien. She was fastening some little blue ribbon bows on the corners of a pin-cushion which Araminta was to take in the next basket, but she performed the trivial task with the same expression with which she would have signed documents of state. She had been a school-teacher for nearly forty years, and she was stiffened into her old attitude of life.

"I don't see as she has," assented the cousin. "Of course she has aged in her looks — she was a real pretty girl — but that's something that can't last forever on this earth." She sighed, and then smiled at an inward conviction that she herself had held her looks better than Araminta, although she was older.

"Of course," replied Sarah, "I know Araminta don't look quite as she did when she was a girl, though I don't suppose I realize that as you would."

"No, of course you wouldn't, but other ways she seems about the same, just as young, only, as near as I can remember, she used to be a little soberer, not quite so lively. She's got a real happy disposition, hasn't she?"

"Yes, she has," replied Sarah, with fervor.

"I declare I never saw anybody any happier, and —"

"And what?" inquired Sarah, suspiciously.

"Nothing, only at first glance I shouldn't be able to see exactly what she had to make her so mighty happy as she seems to be. She ain't any younger, and she's lost her pretty looks, though she's really good-looking; still, you know —"

"Beauty don't amount to much for a woman; when she gets older she'd be silly to fret over that," Sarah said, rather shortly. She had always been distinctly homely herself.

"That's very true," the cousin replied, smiling again over the comfortable reflection concerning her own looks. Martha Spear had been a beauty, and she was, in a florid, middle-aged fashion, a beauty still, with sparkling black eyes, pink cheeks, and smooth crinkles of black hair. "She isn't any too well, either, is she?" she added.

"No, she isn't. She has the hay-fever every summer, and not a winter but she has more or less rheumatism. She was awake half last night with a pain in her shoulder."

"I guess she's worked too steady over these Christmas things."

"I shouldn't wonder, but there's no stopping her. She takes a sight of comfort over them."

"She has a real happy disposition," remarked the cousin again. "And I can't see —" She hesitated again a minute.

"You can't see as she's anything so wonderful to make her happier than other folks?" said Sarah.

"Well, no, to tell you the truth, Sarah, I can't." The cousin laughed apologetically. "Of course, she's got a good, comfortable home here. She has all the comforts of life, and she has you to live with, but —"

"You mean she never got married," said Sarah, bluntly, with a slight tone of defiance.

"I don't suppose she cared to get married, or she would have," the cousin hastened to respond.

"No, she didn't care to get married," Sarah said, with dignified emphasis, "or she would have. Araminta had a chance."

"Of course, I knew she must have," said the cousin, eagerly. "Of course, Araminta was so pretty-looking —"

"She didn't have but one chance, if she was pretty, but she did have one chance," said Sarah, firmly.

"Oh, of course I knew she must have had."

"And she gave up the chance, and she's seemed a good deal happier ever since," said Sarah.

"Well, I never!" said the cousin, in some amazement. "Do you mind tellin' me who it was?" she asked, with thinly veiled eagerness.

"Well, no, I don't know as I do. He don't live here now, nor any of his folks. It happened after you got married and went away."

"Yes, it must have. Araminta is younger than I. She hadn't quite grown up enough for a beau when I was married."

"Well, she got one as soon as she was grown up enough; there wasn't any waiting," said Sarah, with pride.

"Who was it? Anybody I know?"

"Well, I think you must have known him. It was Daniel Rodgers."

"My, yes. Of course I used to know him. He was about my age. I went to school with him. Why, he was pretty smart, wasn't he? His father had money."

"Yes, his father had a good deal of money, and Daniel was the only child. Araminta knew he was coming in for a good deal, but she didn't think of that a second. Some girls might have, but she didn't. He was real smart, too."

"He studied law with Lawyer Clark, didn't he?"

"Yes, and he had set up his office with him. Lawyer Clark was kind of out of health; he didn't live long afterward, and Daniel would have had a good practice if he'd stayed right along here. But as soon as his father died he moved away to the city and set up business there. I hear he's done very well. I think he's a judge."

"He was good-looking, too, as I remember."

"Good-looking! He was handsome — as handsome a fellow as I ever saw. There wasn't a young man in the village to compare with him in looks or appearance."

"And Araminta didn't take a fancy to him?" inquired the cousin, with wonder.

"Yes, she took a fancy to him; at least she did at first. It wasn't that, poor child. No, I won't say poor child. She wasn't poor a mite about it after she'd given him up."

"She gave him up?"

"Yes. See here, Martha. I don't know why I shouldn't tell you about it. It's all over and gone. I haven't ever spoken of it to a soul; nobody in this village has ever dreamed of it. I suppose they've always thought Araminta never had a chance. Let 'em think so. I don't care, and as for Araminta, she's never given it a thought. But I'd just as lief one of our folks knew how it really was — how Araminta never got married — but she had as good a chance and better than most girls here, and she would have been married if she hadn't been so good that she would have made a better wife than any other girl here."

"Araminta would have made a man a beautiful wife," assented the cousin.

"I guess she would, and Daniel Rodgers knew it, too. He had a pretty long head."

"Yes, I always thought he had."

"He had. Well, he begun coming to see Araminta when she wasn't over eighteen. She always seemed older, though. Araminta was real womanly. She didn't seem to have any of the silly ways of most young girls. She knew what she did know, and she knew what she didn't know, and she was real strong on that last knowledge. She was a good housekeeper, young as she was. She took right hold; you know I was school-teaching, and mother wasn't very well. It was three years after father died. You know we had just about enough to live on that he left us, and then my school-teaching money was extra. We never kept any help; Araminta did all the work, and she made all the clothes. She did dress tasty, too. She was as pretty as a picture, too, if I do say it. I've seen young men turn to look after her a good many times, though Daniel

Rodgers was the only one that really went with her. Sometimes I used to think that Araminta was too pretty and too ladylike and too good, that she sort of scared them off. I think there is such a thing. Men want a girl more like themselves. Still, there weren't many young men here."

"No, there weren't, especially young men," assented the cousin.

"That may have been one reason," said Sarah. "Anyhow, Daniel Rodgers was the only one. He begun calling here, and going home with her from meeting, and it was some time before I thought he meant anything, and I knew she didn't feel sure for a long time, and neither did mother. I know once she said, when I was joking her, 'I tell you what it is, Sarah, a fellow has got to be pretty pointed in his attentions before I think they are serious.' Of course, she knew she was pretty-looking, and mother and I did, but I think on that very account we felt a little more distrustful, for a young man is so often attracted by a pretty face for a little while, and then he gets over it as sudden as he begun. Of course, there was a good deal more to Araminta than a pretty face, but the question was whether or not that was what made him take a notion to her.

"He called first one Wednesday evening, then the week after he walked home with her from Friday-evening prayer-meeting. Then a week from the next Sunday he came and spent the evening, then after that he came pretty steady. 'He really is going with you, isn't he?' I said to Araminta, after it had been kept up about six weeks; and she sort of colored up and laughed, and I saw that she had begun to think so. Mother and I talked a good deal about it together, and finally we thought that he really did think a good deal of Araminta, and it wasn't merely a notion to a pretty face. We thought Daniel Rodgers was a young man who had an eye for something besides a pretty face, that he could see the true worth as well. And I really think now that he did, only — well, he had an eye for something else, too. He was like most men, after all. Once in a while you think you see a man who isn't like most men, and maybe once in a dog's age he isn't, but the rest of the time it turns out he is. Daniel Rodgers was. I guess it was Araminta's looks attracted him more than anything else. Well, he had been going with Araminta nearly a year, and it was coming Christmas, and we had begun to think of their being married in June. Araminta seemed just as happy. I don't think she has ever been happy in the same way since, but she has been as happy, and happier, I guess, in another way. I guess she was thinking more about herself then than she ever has since. There was talk about Daniel building a house, though Araminta would rather have planned to live with mother and me. She said she couldn't see how we were going to get along without her. We couldn't quite afford to keep help, and mother wasn't strong enough to do much, and I didn't have much time out of school, except in the summer vacation. She had planned a good deal; well, the plans didn't ever come to anything."

"Didn't folks in the village know about it?" asked the cousin.

"Well, no, they didn't. And now you mention it, I will say that was the one thing mother and I didn't like about the way Daniel managed things. For some reason he didn't want anything said about his and Araminta's being engaged. He said he'd always thought it was better not to let anybody know till the wedding invitations were out, but of course that was no reason at all. Araminta thought it was all right — she hasn't a suspicious streak in her — but mother and I talked it over a good deal."

"Folks must have talked," said the cousin. "They knew he was going with Araminta, didn't they?"

"Yes, they did and they didn't. He used to come calling pretty late, after dark, and after the first he didn't go to prayer-meeting very often to go home with her. And it was very seldom he took her to a concert or lecture in the town hall. Mother and I used to think it was kind of funny that he didn't. Of course, folks talked and said they were going together, but they couldn't really say that they knew anything. Then, too, Daniel was a young man who had always called round at different houses a good deal, and he did after he was going with Araminta. Of course, he didn't call steady at any one place, so far as we knew, but we knew of his calling a good deal. He used to call on the Adams girls, and on Kate Slocum and her aunt. He used to tell us of it himself. Yes, folks talked and surmised, but they didn't really know anything, not even how much he came to see Araminta, and it was lucky afterward for her that they didn't. It made it a good deal easier for her. I don't know what she would have done if she'd thought folks pitied her, were looking and spying and pitying her. I guess that would have been too much even for Araminta.

"Well, the day before Christmas came a beautiful present from Daniel for Araminta. She had been working hard on one, or rather two, for him — a lovely pair of slippers with a letter D in a little wreath of roses on each toe, filled in with brown, and the handsomest crocheted scarf I ever laid my eyes on. You remember when men wore those great scarfs crocheted of worsted, years ago?"

"Yes, I remember."

"Well, that scarf was very long and wide, a pretty red color, and on each end was worked a stag's head and some green leaves. It was an elegant thing, and all the style then, and Araminta had worked real hard making it. His present for her came the day before Christmas, as I said. It was a most beautiful fan, white satin, all painted with roses, and spangled, with feathers on the edge, carved ivory sticks, and little looking-glasses on each end stick. I had never seen anything like it, and Araminta she was so pleased she didn't know what to do. She kept opening the box and looking at it. 'It seems as if it was too nice for me,' says she, 'and he was too extravagant,' and she was all kind of smiling and trembling at the same time, and her cheeks were pink. I remember just how she looked gazing at that fan. She looked pretty enough to kiss. Well, she had just put the fan in the box for the dozenth time, and she had put it away in the chimney cupboard. 'I am not going to waste any more time over that fan,' says she, laughing just as happy. 'I sha'n't get this tidy done if I do,' says she. She was working a tidy for Daniel's aunt, Harriet Ackley, and had to finish it that day. The tidy was crocheted of red and white and green worsted, in stripes; then the stripes were sewed together and worked with flowers in cross-stitch. I remember just as well how that tidy looked. Harriet Ackley had it on a high rocking-chair in her parlor the last I knew. I guess it's there still. Araminta was working the last green stripe with some pink rosebuds, sitting by the south sitting-room window in the sun, just as happy, when we saw that girl come flying up the road."

"What girl?" cried the visiting cousin, eagerly.

"Her name was Grace Ormsby; she came from Bondville. I don't know whether you ever knew her. She was a good deal younger. She wasn't quite so old as Araminta."

"Wasn't she Silas Ormsby's daughter — and she had a sister Louisa?"

"Yes, that's the one."

"Well, I didn't know her, but I remember seeing her sister quite a number of times; she was married before I was. They were quite well off."

"Yes, Silas Ormsby was a rich man; and Grace wasn't pretty, but she was a real good girl and had real taking ways.

"Well, we saw this girl running up the road as if she was possessed. Her coat wasn't fastened and her hood (girls wore hoods that winter; she had a lovely red one) was half off her head, and she hadn't a thing on her hands — it was a bitter day, too. The sun was shining, and the wind blowing from the north, and the air was all full of driving snow that cut like diamond dust. It had snowed the day before, and the high wind swept it all up like a broom. Well, we saw this girl coming, plunging through the snow in the road (the sidewalk wasn't cleared) in a fierce, weak kind of fashion. She had her head down, and she went on as if nothing could stop her, and yet she sort of staggered.

"'Do look at this girl coming,' says I to Araminta, and she looked.

"'Who in the world is it?' says she.

"'I never set eyes on her before,' says I. 'She looks kind of queer. I wonder if anybody's sick and she's going for the doctor?'

"'She can hardly walk, poor thing,' says Araminta. Then she cries out, dreadful astonished, 'Why,' says she, 'she's coming in here!' And she was. That girl turned right in at our front gate. 'It's lucky I swept the path out this morning,' says Araminta, 'or she couldn't have got in at all; but it's blown in a good deal since.'

"'Who is it?' says I, kind of bewildered, peeking around the edge of the window.

"'I don't know,' says Araminta, jumping up and going to open the door, 'but she can hardly walk, poor thing, whoever she is. I'm sorry the snow has blown in on the path so. I don't know but I'd better get the broom and sweep it off again so she can get in.'

"And Araminta did. The snow had blown in on the front walk pretty bad, and Araminta got the broom and ran out and swept away some so the girl could get in without wading up to her knees. I went to the door and stood there with a shawl over my head.

"'Are you Miss Araminta White?' I heard the girl kind of gasp out, while Araminta was swishing the broom in front of her. She stood as if she was going to melt right down like a snow image the next minute, and I could see that her face in the red hood was white as a sheet, and she had a kind of breathless look.

"'Yes,' says Araminta, sweeping away. 'I'm real sorry the path isn't better. I swept it out this morning, but the wind blows so the snow flies right back about a fast as I can sweep it off.' And it did, sure enough. Both those girls stood there in a kind of whirlpool of snow, all glittering and glistening like a rainbow. Araminta was laughing real pleasant, making her broom fly as fast as she could, and the girl stood as if she was just about sinking down. 'There,' says Araminta, in a minute. 'Now I guess you can get in a little better,' and she moves ahead with her broom and the girl tries to follow. But the first thing I knew she staggered and Araminta had dropped the broom and was hanging on to her.

"'What's the matter?' I cried out. I was scared.

"'I guess she's faint,' says Araminta. 'Suppose you get a glass of the blackberry wine, Sarah.' Araminta was half dragging the girl up the walk. Her hood was on her neck by that time and her head was lopping, and she did look ghastly.

"'Can you get her up the steps?' I sings out. And Araminta said she could, and she did; but I never knew how she managed, for the girl was as big as she was and 'most as heavy. I ran down cellar and got a bottle of blackberry wine. It was ten years old, and real strong. There's some left now. I'll give you some."

"I love blackberry wine," said the cousin. "Did the girl faint away?"

"No, not quite. When I got up-stairs Araminta had her hood and coat off and she was lying on the sofa. She kept trying to get up, though she didn't look as if she could sit up a second. She acted dreadful kind of nervous. Araminta was trying to keep her down. 'Just lie still till you feel a little better,' she was saying. 'You are all tuckered out wading through the deep snow.'

"'I want to get up,' says the girl, kind of wild.

"I poured out a good swig of that blackberry wine in a tumbler and I went up to her. 'Here, drink this,' says I, 'and then you'll feel better and you can get up.'

"She looked up at me dreadful pitiful and sort of dazed; a real good little face she had, not pretty a bit, but good, with nice, soft, brown eyes and hair. She looked like a real sweet, obedient little girl, and sensible enough, if she didn't get to thinking too much of a man, and he didn't treat her fair, and that made a fool of her. She was white and forlorn-looking, poor child. I pitied her from the bottom of my heart, though I was out of patience with her, too. For my part, I have never seen how any woman could lose her pride enough to go on the way she did over a mortal man. I've never seen any man that was worth it. Daniel Rodgers wasn't, though he wasn't a bad young man, only too much like other men when it came to a pretty face.

"Well, just a soon as she had swallowed that blackberry wine up she jumped; Araminta couldn't keep her down a minute longer. She was up on her two little feet, thin shoes and no rubbers in all that snow! If she had had a mother I guess she would never have come out in that fashion, man or no man! Her mother was dead, and her aunt, her father's sister, had brought her up. She was kind of flighty, from all I've heard."

"Yes, she was," assented the cousin, with a nod.

"And her sister had just married and gone away to live, and

her father was in the city on business. He never knew about it, I guess. I don't know what he would have done. I've always heard he was a pretty stern sort of man."

"So have I."

"I guess he never knew of it. I know Araminta and I never lisped a word about it, and I don't believe the girl did. I guess she had sense enough for that."

"What did she do?"

"Well, she just stood up and ran to the mantel-shelf, where there was a picture of Daniel Rodgers in a shell frame. Araminta had made the frame herself out of some shells she'd picked up on Barr Beach the summer before. She spent a week there in August. It was a real pretty frame. The shells were stuck in putty. It's in the parlor now, with a picture of a Madonna that one of her Sunday-school scholars gave her in it. Well, that girl she made straight for that picture, and she stood looking at it dreadful wild and pitiful. 'It's true, then,' says she; then, all at once, in a voice so sharp it didn't seem as if it could come from such a mild little mouth, 'I know it's true now,' says she, and she shakes her head and she looks at Araminta.

"Araminta turned kind of pale, but she didn't lose her self-control. She spoke as calm and even as a clock. 'What is it that you know is true?' says she. And she moves close to the girl and puts her hand on her shoulder. The girl sort of pulls away from her at first, for all the world like a sulky baby. Then all of a sudden her arms went round Araminta's neck and her head was on her shoulder, and she was crying to break her heart with her face hidden.

"Then Araminta she patted her head and spoke real soothing. 'What is it, dear?' says she. 'What is the matter?' But the girl just sobbed and sobbed. 'What is it, dear?' says Araminta again.

"Then the girl raised her head and stood off a little way, and looked at Araminta with her poor little face all of a quiver, and the tears streaming and her mouth all puckered up. 'I had him first,' says she, and the tears came again.

"'Had who first?' says Araminta.

"'Daniel,' sobs the girl — 'Daniel.'

"'Do you mean Daniel Rodgers was going with you before he went with me?' says Araminta, and she spoke sterner than I had ever heard her.

"'Yes,' says the girl. 'Yes, he was going with me a long time, ever since I was in long dresses. He used to see me home from places. Aunt Clara didn't tell father, and then he used to come to call real often.'

"'When did he come to see you last?' says Araminta.

"'Not since last Christmas-time,' says the girl, and I heard Araminta draw a long breath. I knew what she had been afraid of and had suspected him of for a minute — that he had been to see both of them at the same time; but he wasn't so bad as that. I don't know as he had been so very bad, after all, only Araminta's pretty face had been a little too much for his faithfulness, because he was nothing but a man. He hadn't been very open, but I suppose he thought the least said soonest mended; and maybe he hadn't been actually engaged to Grace Ormsby, after all, though she thought so, and he must have given her a good deal of reason to think he was serious.

"Well, she began to cry again, and Araminta stood looking at her, and I must say she had a beautiful expression. She was smiling. I didn't see how she could fetch a smile, but she did. 'You thought Daniel liked you?' says she.

"'Yes,' sobs the girl, 'he did. He used to like me better than anybody till — till he saw you.' Then she sobs out loud. 'Oh, oh, it's 'most Christmas,' says she, 'and I can't bear it; I can't, can't! I won't have any present from him, and — last Christmas he — gave me such a beautiful box of candy and a gold pin. Now I sha'n't have any present from him this year. Oh, I wouldn't have come if it hadn't been Christmas. I couldn't bear it. The thinking of last Christmas, how happy I was, and this — I sha'n't have any present from him.'

"'Perhaps you will,' says Araminta.

"'No, I sha'n't,' sobs the girl. 'He'll — he'll give you the present this year!'

"Thinks I, 'What would she say if she were to see that fan?'

"I knew Araminta was thinking about it. Then Araminta kind of started back, as if she couldn't help it, for all of a sudden the girl ran to her again, and snuggled up to her, and cried on her shoulder.

"'Oh, you wouldn't have taken him away if you had known how much I loved him and how I had him first, would you?' says she, for all the world like a child.

"'No,' says Araminta, 'I wouldn't.'

"'I don't see why he left me for you,' says the girl. 'You are better-looking, but I didn't think that was what Daniel looked at more than anything else. I didn't think he was that kind of man, and he isn't, either; and you couldn't possibly love him any better than I do; and I am a pretty good housekeeper, and I was trying very hard to improve. Are you a very good scholar?'

"'Not so very,' says Araminta, and she actually laughed a little.

"'I thought maybe you were and that was the reason he liked you,' says the girl. 'Daniel is such a scholar! I guess you must be more capable than I am, though I have tried very hard to be capable since Daniel began going with me. Are you so very capable?'

"'No, I guess not very,' says Araminta, but she spoke as if she wasn't thinking of what she was saying.

"Then I speaks up for the first time. 'Yes, you are capable, too,' says I; 'you know you are capable.'

"'Then that is the reason,' says the girl, and she sobs and sobs and clings to Araminta.

"I was getting out of patience. It seemed to me I had never seen such goings-on. 'Why don't you and she sit down, Araminta?' says I. 'You will be all tired out.'

"Araminta looks over the girl's head and smiles, and shakes her head at me that I must not interfere. So I didn't say anything more, though I wanted to.

"'You don't know, you don't know,' says the girl, sort of moaning — it was dreadful painful — 'how terrible it has all been. I've watched and watched for him to come, and I wondered and wondered if he was going with any other girl, and I couldn't find out; I didn't know anybody from here besides Daniel. Once I walked 'way over here one moonlight evening. Father and Aunt Clara thought I had gone to meeting. I went to the house where he lives. I hid behind the hedge till he came out, and then I crept out and was going to follow him, but I was so afraid he would turn round and see me that I didn't dare. I went back behind the hedge till he was gone. Then I went home. I ran 'most all the way. I was afraid.'

"'It is five miles to Bondville,' says Araminta, in the kindest voice.

"'Yes,' says the girl. 'I walked ten miles that night. Then I cried till morning. I didn't sleep any. Father and Aunt Clara say they don't see why I have grown so thin.' She was thin, sure enough, poor child. Her little hands were like claws.

"'You walked 'way over here to-day?' says Araminta.

"'Yes,' says the girl, 'but I don't know why I did.' Then she cries out, real hysterical: 'Oh, why did I come! Why did I come! How shall I ever get home!'

"'I am going to take you home,' says Araminta. 'The stage goes over at eleven o'clock, and I will go with you. Nobody need know.

I shall not get out of the stage.'

"'Oh, will you?' says the girl, and she clung to her tighter than ever. She was a queer kind of a creature. I don't believe many girls would have taken it the way she did.

"Then Araminta spoke real firm. 'Now,' says she, 'I want you to sit down here in the chair beside the stove. And I am going to make a good, hot cup of tea and cook you an egg and make you some toast. Have you eaten any breakfast?'

"'No, I haven't,' says the girl. 'I couldn't. Aunt Clara wanted to know why, but I wouldn't tell her. I guess she suspected.'

"Well, she did just as Araminta told her to. She sat down by the stove, and Araminta got a good, hot breakfast for her, and she ate it, too. She was just about worn out. I made her take off her soaking-wet shoes and stockings, and got some slippers of Araminta's for her while they dried. It was nearly an hour before the stage went.

"Well, I never knew how Araminta managed it, or just what she said, but she got the girl all quieted down and she went off with her real calm.

"Araminta was gone about an hour and a half. She just went over in the stage and turned round and came back again. I don't think anybody ever knew anything about it. She said there weren't any other passengers over to Bondville that morning. There were two coming back.

"When Araminta came into the room I couldn't bear to look at her at first. I could hear her moving about taking off her things. 'Dinner is all ready when you are,' says I. I didn't look at her when I said it. I had been getting dinner while she was gone.

"But she spoke just as natural. 'I'm all ready now,' says she, 'and I am hungry, too. I smelled the beefsteak the minute I came into the yard.'

"Then I looked at her, and she was just as usual. I didn't know what to say. We went out in the other room, and I took the beef-steak out of the oven and she took up the potatoes.

"'Well, what are you going to do?' says I when we sat down, and I could hear my voice shake.

"'I am going to make a Christmas present,' says Araminta, and she laughed just as pleasant.

"'To that girl?' says I.

"'Yes,' says she.

"'What?' says I.

"'A man and a fan,' says Araminta, and then she laughed again.

"She didn't?" said the cousin.

"Yes, she did," replied Sarah, "in spite of all I could say; and I did say a good deal, when it came right down to it. There I was, not married, and — Well, I've always thought it was the right way for a woman to be married, if she could, and I wanted her to be happy. But she wouldn't listen to anything I said. She just laughed, and said she was bound to be happy anyway. She would always have a good deal to be thankful for, and she knew she would be happy. I told her maybe she'd never have another chance, and she said if she did she'd never take it; but she never did have one."

"Well, marriage ain't everything," said the cousin.

"No," said Sarah; "it isn't so much as giving it up and behaving yourself, if the Lord shows He hasn't planned to have you married."

"That's what Araminta did?"

"Yes, that's what Araminta did."

"But," said the cousin, "I don't see how she managed to give away Daniel and the fan to the other girl."

"That was easy enough," said Sarah. "She did up that fan and sent it to Grace Ormsby. She didn't send any card or anything; she knew the girl would jump at thinking he had sent it. Then she sends a note to Daniel, saying she won't be home Christmas, and off she goes and spends Christmas with her cousin Alice in Fayetteville. She'd told Grace to send him a little note asking him to call on her Christmas evening, and he went. Araminta thought she could count on it. She reasoned it out that he would be real huffy because she had gone off without a word to him, and when he heard from Grace he would be glad enough to go, and when he saw her the old feeling would come over him again — that is, if it had ever been worth anything — and she was right. And I suppose when he saw Grace Ormsby with the fan he had sent to Araminta he gave Araminta up on the spot."

"I wonder if Grace Ormsby ever knew about the fan," said the cousin.

"I rather guess not," said Sarah. "Sometimes Araminta has felt kind of uneasy about her course with that fan, as if maybe she was sort of underhanded, but it turned out all right, and she really felt as if the other girl was the one to have it. Anyway, it settled him as far as Araminta was concerned. Pretty soon we heard he was going with Grace Ormsby, then pretty soon they got married and went away to live. I hear she has made him a very good wife. Once Araminta said to me that unless she had been quite sure that she would, she should have hesitated more than she did. She said it seemed to her that Grace Ormsby would make him very happy."

"I think Araminta seems happy enough herself without him," said the cousin.

"Yes, I guess she did just as well to let him go," replied Sarah. "He was a smart man, but she's been just as well off in a good many ways. Here she is now." Then Araminta entered, and again stood in the doorway with her basket empty of presents. "Look at her," said her sister, with a sort of tender pride. "Don't she look happy, Martha?"

"I never saw anybody take so much comfort in giving Christmas presents in all my life," said the cousin.

Araminta laughed. "Sometimes it seems to me as if I was emptying all the baskets into my own heart and didn't really give anything," said she.

THE BUTTERFLY

"It's time for Vilola to come home again, and B. F. Brown is havin' paintin' and paperin' done," said Mrs. Abner Wells to her sister. Her sister's name was Mrs. Francis Baker, and she had come over with her work and her baby to spend the afternoon.

"Well, I thought there was something goin' on there when I came past," responded Mrs. Baker. "I noticed that the front chamber windows were open, and I saw some old room-paper flyin' round the yard."

"The man just finished it — went away since dinner."

"That front room is Vilola's, ain't it?"

"Yes, of course it is. Didn't you know it?"

"Why, when did he have that room papered before?"

"He had it papered only the last time she came," said Mrs. Wells, impressively.

"Why, that couldn't have been more'n a year ago."

"Of course it couldn't. Don't Vilola Brown always come once a year and spend six months with her father, and then go back to Jefferson and spend six months with her mother? Ain't she done that ever since her father and mother separated when she was a baby? I should think you might know that as well as I do, Elmira Baker."

"Oh, of course I do," said Mrs. Baker; "I was only talking at random. I was only wondering what he was having that room papered for if it was done only a year ago."

"Well, I can tell you," said Mrs. Wells, with asperity. "Some folks have money to throw away for nothing, or think they do. They may find out they don't have any more than some other folks in the long run. I can tell you why. When we had that heavy spell of rain last fall it leaked in that room around the chimney and there was a place about as big as a saucer stained, that's why."

"Was that all?"

"Yes, that was all. B. F. Brown ain't goin' to have his precious Vilola comin' home to sleep in a room that's got a spot on the paper, if it ain't any bigger than the head of a *pin*. I don't know what he thinks that girl is."

"Couldn't he have had the paper pieced?"

"Oh no. It was faded just a little. He wouldn't have *Vilola* sleep in a room with a patch of paper showin'. I *guess* he wouldn't."

"Now, Susan, you don't mean he's so silly as that?"

"Yes, I do. I had it from the woman he's been having to clean the house. I tell you that house has been cleaned from attic to cellar. Every carpet has been up. Well, it needed it bad enough. I don't believe it had been swept since Vilola went away last July."

"I wonder if B. F. Brown makes much money in his store?" said Mrs. Baker.

"I don't believe he makes much," said Mrs. Wells, with angry exultation. "I know lots of folks that won't trade there. They say he never has just what they want. They say Deering, and Lawton, or Hapgood & Lewis have a great deal better assortment. I ain't been inside the door since I bought my brown cashmere there, and it faded so after I'd only wore it six months, and he wouldn't allow me anything for it. I told him then it was the last trading I'd do in his store, and it *was* the last."

"I wonder if she's comin' to-night?" said Mrs. Baker.

"No, she ain't comin' to-night. The six months with her mother ain't up till next-week Thursday. I've kept account."

"It's a queer way for folks to live, ain't it?" said Mrs. Baker. "I rather *think* it's queer."

"How long is it since they've lived together? I declare, I've forgot."

"*I* ain't forgot. Vilola Brown is just seven years younger than I be. She's nineteen, and her father and mother ain't lived together since she was three years old. That makes sixteen years. I was ten years old when they separated and her mother went to Jefferson to live, and he stayed here, and one had Vilola six months and the other six months, turn and turn about, ever since, and he's paid his wife ten dollars a week all this time, and nobody knows how much Vilola has cost him. She's had everything, and she's never raised her finger to earn a penny herself."

"What do you 'spose the trouble was?"

"Well, they were dreadful close-mouthed, but I guess it was pretty well known at the time what the matter was. I've heard mother talk about it with the neighbors. Mrs. B. F. Brown had an awful temper, and so has B. F. They couldn't get along together."

"There wasn't anything against her, was there?"

"No, I never heard a word against her. She was a dreadful pretty woman. I can just remember how she looked. It was when they used to wear curls, and she had real feathery light ones, and the pinkest cheeks, and used to dress real tasty, too. I guess folks sided with her pretty generally. I don't believe B. F. Brown has ever stood quite so well here as he did before."

"Vilola don't take much after her mother, does she?"

"No, she don't. There ain't a homelier girl anywheres around than Vilola Brown, and she hasn't got a mite of style about her, either."

B. F. Brown was rather laboriously making milk toast for supper. By dint of long practice he could make milk toast, griddle-cakes, and fry a slice of meat or fish and boil a potato. He was not an expert at any household tasks, though he had served long, having an unusual measure of masculine clumsiness. Although he was not a large man, his fingers were large, with blunt, round ends. He had no deftness of touch. He burned himself seeing if the toast was brown, and finally burned the toast. When the meal was ready he called the cat, which was asleep in a round, yellow ring of luxurious comfort beside the stove. The cat rose lazily at his summons, rounding its back and stretching. The cat belonged to Vilola, and he cherished it like a child during the six months of her absence with her mother. "If anything happened to that cat, I don't know what my daughter would say," he told his clerk, John Bartlett. B. F. Brown kept a small dry-goods store on the village Main Street, and John Bartlett, who was as old as himself and had been with him ever since he was in business, and a boy constituted his entire force of trade.

"I should think she would have to take the cat with her when she goes to stay with her mother, she thinks so much of her," replied John Bartlett. The conversation had taken place upon the occasion of a temporary loss and recovery of the cat.

"Oh, she has got another cat she keeps there, a tiger," said B. F. Brown; "she leaves him there when she comes here; but she don't think near so much of him as she does of this yellow one."

To-night, as B. F. Brown placed a saucer filled with a share of his own supper on the floor beside the stove for the cat, he talked to it with a pitiful, clumsy, masculine crooning: "Poor Kitty, poor kitty. There now; eat your supper, Kitty."

"Guess that pussy-cat will be glad to see her," he muttered, as he sat down to his own supper. Every now and then as he ate he paused, with his fork suspended half-way to his mouth with a bit of toast, and looked upward with an ecstatic expression. His soul was tasting to the full such a savor of anticipatory happiness that he had small comprehension of physical sensations. After he had finished supper he washed his dishes with painful care. He was particular to put every dish in its place on the pantry shelves. He had had the pantry thoroughly cleaned and all the dishes washed and rearranged, and he was fearful lest he disorder them before his daughter arrived. Then he went back to the kitchen and surveyed the clean, shining, yellow surface of the floor anxiously. He had had that newly painted, and he was desperately afraid of marring it before his daughter saw it. He took off his shoes and put on slippers before stepping on it. He kept his slippers in the shed for that purpose and entered through the shed door. He spied a few crumbs on the floor, which he carefully gathered up with his blunted fingers; then he saw a dusty place, which he wiped over with his pocket-handkerchief. He had planned many surprises for his daughter, as he always did on her home-coming. This time he had one which was, in his estimation, almost stupendous. He had purchased a sideboard. Vilola had always talked about a sideboard for the dining-room some time when they got rich. She had never asked for one. That was not Vilola's way. She had seldom asked for anything in her whole life, but her father had taken note and remembered. The week before he had gone about anxiously pricing sideboards. He had saved up a certain amount for one. When he found that he could not only purchase a sideboard with his hoard, but a nice, little rocking-chair for Vilola's room as well, he was jubilant.

He went home whistling under his breath like a boy. He had an idea that there should be a rich display of some sort on a sideboard, and he searched the house for suitable ornaments. He found an old-fashioned glass preserve-dish on a standard, a little painted mug which had been his in babyhood, and a large cup and saucer with "Gift of Friendship" on the front in gold letters. He arranged these in a row on the sideboard with the tall glass dish in the centre. Then he stood off and surveyed the cheap oak piece with its mirror and gaudily carved doors and its decorations doubtfully, not being entirely satisfied.

Then all at once his face lit up. He hastened into his own bed-room out of the sitting-room, and brought forth in triumph his last year's Christmas present from Vilola. It was a brush-and-comb tray decorated with blue roses. He dusted it carefully with his pocket-handkerchief and placed it on the sideboard to the right of the cup and saucer. In the tray were the nice, new brush and comb which had been a part of the present. He had never used them. He thought too much of them for that. He removed the brush and comb and stood for a minute with them in his hand, with his head on one side, surveying the effect of the sideboard without them.

Then he replaced the brush and comb in the tray. He was fully satisfied.

"She'll be tickled 'most to death," he said. He whistled again as he went up-stairs to see Vilola's room. He whistled "Annie Laurie," and the words of the old song floated through his mind in company with the air:

> *"Her brow is like the snow-drift,*
> *Her throat is like the swan, ...*
> *And for bonnie Annie Laurie*
> *I'd lay me down and die."*

His dear daughter Vilola was in his fancy as Annie Laurie. All the romance of his nature, purified and spiritualized, was represented by his daughter.

When he reached her room, the best chamber in the house, the front one with two windows, he set the little lamp which he carried on the shelf and looked about with delight. The new paper was all on. It was a pretty paper — a white ground with a lustre of satin, covered with garlands of blue violets. There was a deep border and a little white-and-gold picture-moulding. This last was something quite new; Vilola had never had a picture-moulding in her room. "I guess she'll like that," he chuckled. He joyously anticipated hanging the pictures the next evening. That evening he had to be in his store. The next day the woman was to put down the carpet in the room and clean the paint and windows. The next evening he himself would give the finishing-touches. Never had he looked forward to any treat as he did to this simple service for the sake of his daughter. Vilola was coming in two days. The day after to-morrow was to be devoted by the woman to cooking. When Vilola was at home the fare was very different from his when alone. Anything was good enough for him, nothing good enough for Vilola.

To-night he stood in the dining-room door and surveyed the sideboard again. It looked more beautiful to him than ever. "It's a grand piece of furniture, and no mistake," he said. Then he sat happily down by the kitchen stove and the cat jumped up in his lap. Suddenly he reflected that a ribbon around the cat's neck would be an appropriate attention. "Want a ribbon bow on your neck when she comes home?" he asked the cat. He stroked the cat, who purred, and the man would have purred had his state of mind been the only essential.

The next morning he bought a great turkey. In the afternoon the house was redolent with savory odors of cooking. The woman who had cleaned the house had come in the morning to put Vilola's room in order, in the afternoon to do the cooking. B. F. had a great store of cakes and pies prepared, and the turkey also was cooked.

He consulted with the woman, and it was agreed that it could be warmed over the next day and be just as good. "I don't want her to have to go right to hard cookin'," he said.

After the woman had gone that night B. F. went about the house viewing the improvements. He gazed blissfully at the loaded pantry shelves. He had refused to touch one of the new pies or cakes for his supper. He and the cat had fared as usual on milk toast.

Then he went up to Vilola's room. The carpet was now down in the room; he had hung the simple pictures, a few photographs, and two or three flower pieces which had come as prizes with periodicals. Everything was in order. The delicate blue-and-white paper was charming. The curtains had been washed and ironed, and hung crisply in ruffling folds of muslin; there was a fresh white cover on the bureau; Vilola's blue pin-cushion had been taken from the top drawer; her father had bought a bottle of violet water, and that stood beside it. There was a clean white counterpane on the bed, and the pillow-shams were stiff surfaces of shiny whiteness. B. F. looked about, and there was something childish in his expression. His joy over his daughter's prospective joy was at once simple, puerile, and almost heavenly in its innocence.

"I guess she'll be pretty pleased," he said, and he whistled going down-stairs.

Vilola was to arrive the next afternoon, B. F. came home from the store about eleven o'clock in the morning. He made a slow fire in the kitchen stove. He put the turkey in the oven. He laboriously prepared the vegetables himself and put them on to boil. He set the table, putting on a clean table-cloth, awry and wrong side out, and, as a crowning glory, he had bought a dozen carnation pinks. These hung sprawling from a tumbler in the centre of the table. He had also bought four pots of geraniums, all in bloom, and these were on a light stand in the sitting-room window. Then he got ready to go to the station to meet Vilola. He shaved, and put on a clean shirt and collar and black tie. He brushed his clothes carefully. His clothes were all that worried him. He really needed a new suit and a new overcoat, but if he had bought them the sideboard and the new paper could not have been bought, unless he had run in debt. B. F. had a horror of debt, even for the gratification of Vilola. He brushed his clothes very carefully, and hoped that Vilola would not feel ashamed of him. The collar of the overcoat troubled him the most, for there were worn places quite white on the velvet. But just before he set out a lucky expedient occurred to him. He got the ink-bottle and smeared the white places with ink. Then he put on the coat and was quite easy in his mind. He did not know that his face and his white collar were smeared with the ink.

He hurried down the street to the railroad station. It was about half a mile away. The air was raw and the sky overcast, and snow threatened. He noticed that and his joy was enhanced. It would snow, and he and Vilola would be so snug in the warm house, with the flowers and all that good fare. Before his eyes moved ever in advance, as he walked, a little picture of home and innocent love and happiness, projected upon the wintry landscape from the inward light of his soul. He bowed radiantly to everybody whom he met. "Hullo, B. F., have you struck oil?" one man asked, jocosely.

"No," replied B. F.; "my daughter is coming on the one-six train."

"Oh!" returned the man, who was on his way home to dinner. When he saw his own daughter, a plump school-girl, he looked at her with a new wonder of tenderness in his eyes. "It would come pretty hard not to see Nellie for six months at a time," he reflected. He knew B. F.'s story — or as much as anybody knew of it.

B. F. reached the station twenty minutes before the arrival of the train. He went into the waiting-room and sat down on a settee, but he did not remain long. He went out on the platform and paced up and down, his overcoat buttoned tightly. The air had the snow-chill. "I hope she's dressed warm," he thought. Every time he reached the forward end of the platform he peered down the track for a first glimpse of the train. "Train ain't due for fifteen minutes," said the village expressman, with friendly importance. "I know it," responded B. F., but he continued to peer down the track. He got a certain pleasure from so doing; he seemed in that manner to be prolonging the delight of seeing the first approach of the train. He was drawing out the sweetness of a passing moment to its full length.

At last the train came in sight. B. F. saw quite distinctly the puff of smoke from the locomotive. He heard the deep panting like the respiration of a giant. His heart leaped; he felt almost a hysterical impulse to tears. Then all at once a terror gripped him. Suppose she had not come, suppose anything had happened? The terror was so convincing that he felt for a second all the pangs of disappointment. The train came to a stop before the station. The people began streaming out. B. F. drew timidly near, incalculable anxiety and suspense in his face superseding joyous expectation. He felt sure that she had not come. Then he saw her coming rather clumsily down the steps of a car, holding her heavy satchel before her. Vilola was inclined to stoutness, although a young girl, and she had not much muscle. B. F. felt that revulsion of spirits which comes from the realization of a longed-for happiness after the dread of disappointment. He sprang forward. "Here you be," he said, in a hoarse voice. He clutched Vilola's satchel, he helped her down the steps. He did not look at her, for he felt his face working, but he felt her pleasant, loving, blue eyes on him. "Well, I am glad to get here," said she, in a sweet, low, droning voice. "I was afraid the snow would come and delay the train. It has been spitting snow half the way. How are you, father?"

"Well — well," replied B. F., in a sort of ecstatic gasp. He seized Vilola by the arm with a sort of fierceness. "She's here," he told himself, defiantly. "She's here; nothing can alter that now. She's here."

When he and Vilola were in the stage-coach — and old-fashioned stage-coach ran to the railroad station — he kept glancing at her with the same exultation, which had in it something challenging. It was as if he said to a hard fate which had hitherto oftener than not pressed him against the wall, "This joy I have, and it cannot be otherwise."

Suddenly Vilola, looking at him, began to laugh. "What *have* you got on your face, father?" said she. "A great, black smirch. Your collar, too." It was the ink. She took her handkerchief and rubbed his face hard. B. F. shut his eyes tightly. She hurt him, but he was blissful. "It won't come off," said she. "We shall have to wait till we get home. You are a sight!" But she looked at him with the tenderest admiration, even as she laughed.

Vilola chattered pleasantly all the way home. She looked out at her father's little dry-goods store on the Main Street with interest. She asked about business. She asked for one and another of the neighbors. "Oh, how glad I am to be home," she kept repeating, in a heartfelt tone like a refrain.

"How did you leave your mother?" B. F. asked, in a peculiar tone — the one he always used on these occasions when inquiring for his wife.

"Oh, mother's real well," replied Vilola, "and she looks younger than ever. She looks young enough to be my daughter. She's as pretty as a picture this winter; she's got a lovely new dress with brown fur on it, and a black hat. Mr. Anderson was in last evening, and he told her she ought to have her picture painted in it. She wore it to church last Sunday. I saw Mr. Anderson looking at her."

"You say Mr. Anderson came in last evening?" asked B. F., quickly.

"Yes," replied Vilola, looking at him with wonder.

"What did he come for?"

"He brought home a magazine that mother had lent Mrs. Anderson. She had kept it 'most a month, and mother hadn't read it herself. Why, what makes you look so, father?"

B. F.'s face had sobered as they jolted along in the stage-coach. Vilola looked at him uneasily. "Why, what's the matter, father," she asked. "What's come over you? Ain't you glad I've come home?"

Then B. F. pulled himself together. He laughed tenderly, and looked at the girl with a beaming face.

"So you think father ain't glad to get you home?" he said. "Well!"

Vilola laughed too. "Well, you looked so solemncholy all at once. I didn't know," said she, with the pretty little pout of a petted creature who can estimate her power with mathematical accuracy. Vilola had been petted by her mother as well as her father. She was a plain girl who gave the effect of prettiness. Her features were not regular; she had a rippling profile and a wide mouth, but her color was beautiful, and so was her thick, soft, light hair puffing over her broad forehead, and she had an expression of arch amiability which was charming. She was rather stout, but daintily built, and dimpled. She had pulled off her gloves, and she had hold of her father's arm with one little plump hand, dented over the knuckles. On one finger shone a small turquoise ring which her father had given her. He looked at it with proprietary delight.

"Haven't lost your ring, have you?"

"No; and everybody admires it. They ask me where I got my ring. They think some fellow gave it to me, and when they say so I laugh and say, 'Yes, the nicest fellow in the whole world gave me that ring,' and then they wonder. Why, it got all around Jefferson that I was engaged, and even mother came to me and asked what it meant. She laughed when I told her. Mother wanted to be remembered to you, father."

"I'm much obliged to her," replied B. F., with gravity.

"How long is it since you've seen mother?" said Vilola.

"Oh, about sixteen years next spring, I guess."

"I guess you'd know her anywhere if you were to see her," said Vilola. "I don't believe she can be changed a mite. She is just as pretty. She looks like a girl."

Vilola spoke with a certain wistfulness. She looked at her

father with an unspoken plea and question in her eyes. He knew what it was — "Oh, father, why don't you go to see mother? Why don't you live together, and let me live with you both, instead of having these partings? Why, father?"

Once she had put her question into words, and her father had answered with a decision and dignity which she had never seen in him before. "Never, as long as you live, ask me that again, Vilola," he had said. "I have done the best I can do for us all." That ended it. Vilola had never spoken on the subject again, but she often looked at him with the question in her eyes.

When the stage-coach drew up in front of B. F.'s little story-and-half cottage where Vilola had been born, and which was more like home to her than any other, more like home than her mother's house inherited from her grandmother, which was more pretentious, the girl dimpled with delight at the sight of the little, familiar place. "Oh, how good it looks!" said she. "I am so glad to get back!" She jumped out of the stage and ran up the path to the door. She danced up and down like a child. She could not wait for her father to unlock the door. "Hurry, hurry!" said she. "I want to get in! I want to see how it looks!"

B. F., looking fairly foolish with rapture, fumbled with the key. He cast a blissfully confidential glance at the man bringing in the trunk, when he straightened himself up and flung open the door, and Vilola flew in before them.

Vilola was in the kitchen doorway, dancing and sniffing. "Oh, I smell something awful good — awful good!" she proclaimed. "I know what it is. You can't cheat me." She raced into the kitchen and opened the oven door. "I knew, I knew!" cried she, with a shout of exultant laughter. "Oh, isn't it great — isn't it great! I'm home, and I'm going to have roast turkey for dinner!"

"I thought you would like it," returned B. F., with a queer little embarrassed pucker of his mouth. He was so happy, so enraptured at the success of his preparations, that he was fairly shamefaced. When he had shut the front door after the man, Vilola had penetrated the dining-room and discovered the new sideboard. She stood with the cat in her arms, gazing at it, then at him, alternately, speechless. He laughed; at the same time he felt the tears in his eyes. "Well," he said, "well!"

Then Vilola spoke. *"Father!"* said she. "Father Brown — If you aren't — I never — a new —" It was disjointed, but the more expressive. Joy at its extreme is not sequential.

"I thought you would like it," said B. F.

"Like it!"

"Do you think it is a pretty one?" asked B. F., anxiously.

"Pretty? Why, father, it is the most beautiful sideboard I ever saw. It is magnificent — just magnificent!"

"I don't know what you'd like on it," said B. F., radiantly. "So I thought I would put a few things on it, and you could fix 'em up when you came. Take 'em off if you don't like 'em."

Vilola's eyes at that moment rested full on the brush-and-comb tray and the brush and comb, but she smiled like an angel at her father — a smile of grateful tenderness which had in it something protecting. "It is all beautiful," said she — "beautiful!"

When Vilola saw her own room and the new paper she was wild with delight. "Oh, it is lovely!" said she. "Lovely! It is prettier than the paper on my room at mother's, and I thought that was lovely."

"I'm real glad it suits you," said B. F.

"It is perfectly lovely, but I didn't need it. Why, the paper on my room at mother's is new, too, and the other in this room was only on six months. You're extravagant, father."

"Oh, it don't cost much," said B. F., "and the other paper was stained pretty bad. It leaked in when it rained."

"The way you and mother spoil me!" said Vilola. "Here both of you have got new paper for my room twice in one year."

"Guess ther ain't much spoiling," said B. F. He did not tell her that it was at his instance that the new paper had been put upon her room at her mother's, and that he had paid for it. Neither did he tell her that the pretty, new suit that she wore had been purchased with money provided by him. Vilola believed that her mother had furnished it from her own income. She had a little income besides the ten dollars a week paid her by her husband.

B. F. Brown had guarded all along his wife's good name so carefully that people, generally speaking, believed in it. There had never been any scandal. People opined that she was a good woman as well as a very pretty one.

B. F.'s wife had been quite a favorite, particularly with men, though there had never been a whisper against her in consequence. Other women never accused her of any indiscretion, though they made insinuations against her temper. B. F. had not so strenuously defended her temper, though he never made voluntary mention of it. Vilola supposed that her mother's temper was the reason of the separation. That day, when she and her father were happily seated at dinner, with the turkey and the bouquet of pinks between them, Vilola, when there came a lull in the conversation, said, with an expression which showed that she had

had it on her mind to say, "Mother and I have been getting on real nice together lately, father."

"I'm glad you have," said B. F.

"I have never seen that mother's temper was so very bad," said Vilola. "Maybe it's better than it was when I was very young."

"Maybe it is," said B. F.

Then he helped Vilola to some turkey, and nothing more was said about the subject. Vilola had had her girlish dreams of bringing about a reconciliation between her parents, but she had always been baffled by both. Her mother had answered her always as her father had done, though with a certain haste and terror instead of his dignified decision. "It ain't best," said she. "It ain't best for us ever to live together. Don't talk any more about it."

Vilola had spent many anxious and speculative hours over the whole situation. She was a girl of strongly developed affections, and she adored both her parents. She had never had a lover. She was not that sort of girl, people said. Vilola never considered the matter much herself.

"The girls say I am going to be an old maid," she told her father. "And I don't know but I am."

"Well, I hope it will turn out the way that is best for you," said B. F.

"It looks to me now as if I would full as soon keep house for you and mother as get married," said Vilola. "I don't know as I care anything about getting married. It looks to me like quite an undertaking."

"Yes, it's apt to be," said B. F., soberly.

Vilola was a good housekeeper; she took genuine delight in it. She and her father lived together very happily during the six months. Occasionally Vilola had a tea-party. The day before she was to leave, the last day of June, when her six months with her father were up, she invited Mrs. Abner Wells and her sister, Mrs. Francis Baker, to tea. It was a beautiful tea, and Vilola had cooked everything herself. The house also, as the visitors said, looked like wax. Mrs. Baker told B. F. Brown that his daughter was a wonderful housekeeper and she had never eaten such biscuits. Brown was radiant with pride and affection. Mrs. Wells had been covertly questioning Vilola all the afternoon, now she turned on her father.

"I guess your daughter takes after her mother," said she, in a sour-sweet voice. "Her mother was a splendid housekeeper, wasn't she?"

"Yes," said B. F., "Vilola's mother *was* a splendid housekeeper.

I guess Vilola *did* take it from her."

"Her mother must have spent a good deal of time teaching her," said Mrs. Wells. This was while Vilola was in the kitchen putting away the tea dishes.

"Yes," said B. F., "she did take a sight of pains with her."

"I just remember your wife," said Mrs. Wells, "and I used to think she was about the prettiest woman. She *was* a real pretty woman, wasn't she?"

"Yes, she was, real pretty," said B. F.

Vilola came in then with some dishes to be put in the parlor china-closet. "Mother's just as handsome now as ever she was," said she, proudly.

"Yes," said B. F., "I'm sure she is."

"She was real tasty, wasn't she, too?" said Mrs. Wells.

"Yes," said B. F., patiently.

"And real pretty spoken?"

"Yes."

"Oh," said Vilola, "mother has got the prettiest ways. Everybody is taken with mother."

"It was always so," said B. F., with a certain fervor.

He even smiled, as if at the contemplation of something pleasant which was before his eyes.

"And she was real kind-hearted, too; I've heard my mother say so," continued Mrs. Wells. "She used to say that Mis' B. F. Brown was always ready to do any little thing for a neighbor when they needed it. She'd lend her table-cloths and napkins when they had company, or her spoons, and if they was short of victuals, and company came unexpected, she'd send over cake or pie just as free. And she was always ready to sit up when anybody was sick. Mother said that she was about the kindest-hearted woman and the most generous she ever saw."

"Yes," assented B. F., with a joyous expression. "Yes, she *was* real kind-hearted and always ready to help anybody."

"She is now," said Vilola, setting away the best cups and saucers in the parlor china-closet.

Mrs. Wells was baffled; she smiled aimlessly, and repeated that she had heard her mother say so. She was relieved when her sister, Mrs. Baker, gave a sudden cry and diverted attention from the subject.

"For goodness' sake, just look at that, will you!" cried Mrs. Baker.

And they all looked at a gorgeous black-and-gold butterfly sailing about the room, and finally pausing over a vase of June roses on the parlor shelf. "Isn't he a beauty?" said Vilola. "I don't know as I ever saw a butterfly in the house before."

"It's a dreadful bad sign, I've always heard," said Mrs. Wells, presagefully.

"A sign of what?" asked Vilola, rather anxiously. She had a vein of superstition.

"I don't know," replied Mrs. Wells; "something dreadful. Mother always used to say it was. It's worse than a bird." She gave a glance at B. F., as if she was rather pleased that a misfortune was on his track. Going home that night she told her sister that she had never seen such a double-faced man as B. F. Brown, treating his poor wife the way he did and yet praising her.

After the guest had left, Vilola sat down beside the open window and looked out on the moonlit night, full of soft, waving shadows and breathing with sweet flower-scents. Her father sat at the other front window, also looking out. Finally, Vilola turned to him.

"Father," said she.

B. F. looked up. "Well?" he replied.

"I can't get something through my head."

"What?"

"I can't get it through my head," said Vilola, quite boldly and simply, "why, when you don't live with mother, and when, of course, you don't think so very much of her, you should say all those nice things about her that you did this evening."

"They were true," said B. F.

"Well, I know that; of course they were true, but — you acted as if you were glad they were true."

B. F. looked out at the moonlit night, and he had an exalted, far-away expression. "Well," he said, "as near as I can tell you, it's something like this: You know about butterflies, don't you, how there's always a butterfly comin' out of the worm and that little case they crawl into?"

"Why, yes," replied Vilola, wonderingly.

"Well," said B. F., in a tone at once shamed and sublime, "I've about come to the conclusion that there's always a butterfly, or something that's got wings, that comes from everything, and if you look sharp you'll see it, and there can't anything hinder your havin' that, anyhow, and — mebbe that's worth more than all the rest."

"Oh," said Vilola.

B. F. said no more. He gazed out of the window again, and his face shone in the moonlight. Vilola kept glancing at him. His forehead was knitted perplexedly; her eyes showed a furtive alarm. This speech of B. F.'s was at variance with anything which her New England training had led her to expect. A vague terror of and admiration for her father seized her. "What made him say that?" she kept repeating to herself, even after she was in bed. Her trunk was all packed, for she was going in the morning. She was sorry to go, and her heart was sore with pity for her father to be left alone, but she reflected with joy upon the prospect of seeing her mother. She was going on an earlier train than usual; she usually did not leave until night, arriving in Jefferson the next morning. This time she would travel part of the way by day, and reach her destination about midnight. She had not advised her mother of her change of plan. "I guess mother will be surprised," she told her father, when he was seeing her off at the station the next day.

"Now, I don't feel very easy about your getting there at midnight and nobody there to meet you," said B. F. "Hadn't I better send a telegram to your mother?"

"If you do I shall be dreadfully disappointed," said Vilola. "I've set my heart on surprising mother. There's always a carriage at the midnight train; and it isn't five minutes from the station. Promise you won't telegraph, father."

"Well," said B. F., and then the train came.

B. F.'s heart was heavy going home alone. It was noon, and he had not had any dinner. He had a vague idea of eating something before he went to the store, but he sat down beside the kitchen window and remained there a half-hour. It was cool for July. He gazed out at the green yard. There was a cherry-tree full of red fruit, and the robins were clamoring in it. Vilola was fond of the cherries. Yesterday afternoon he had had some picked for her, and she had carried a basketful away. B. F. gazed at the cherry-tree. He could not bear to look at the empty room behind him. He could hear the tick of the clock, and it sounded like the very voice of loneliness. He took out his handkerchief and put it to his eyes, and bent his head, and his narrow, elderly shoulders shook a little. His bowed gray head looked patient and pathetic. Presently he rose and went to the store without eating anything.

The next day, about six o'clock in the afternoon, a thunderstorm was gathering in the northwest. B. F. started for home, and he walked rather quickly in order to reach shelter before the storm broke. The northwest was a livid black with copper lights. There was a confluent mutter of thunder. B. F. came in sight of his house, and saw, to his amazement, that the front chamber windows were open. He had thought they were closed as usual when Vilola went away. He smelled smoke, and, looking up, saw a thin spiral of blue curling out of the kitchen chimney. A sudden alarm seized him. His knees trembled as he hurried around to the kitchen door. The door stood open. There was an odor of tea. B. F. gasped. He entered tremulously. As he did so there was a blue flash of lightning in the room, then there was a sharp fusillade of thunder. Vilola came running out of the dining-room. "Oh, I'm so glad you've come," said she. "It's going to be a terrible tempest."

B. F. gazed at her. He strove to speak, but he only stammered.

Vilola looked at him quite firmly, though she was very pale, and there was a curious, shocked expression in her blue eyes. "Yes," said she, "I've come back."

B. F. continued to look at her.

"Yes," said Vilola, "I'm never going to live with mother again."

Suddenly, as she said mother, a burning, painful red flushed her face and neck.

"Yes, I guess you had better live with me all the time now," said B. F. There came another blue flash of blinding light, a tremendous jar of thunder, then the rain roared past the windows. "I've left my chamber windows open, and my new paper will be wet!" cried Vilola, as she ran. The teakettle on the stove boiled over with a furious sputter. B. F. rose and set it back. Then he stood staring absently out of the window at the flooding of the rain which was washing off some of the dust of the world.

THE LAST GIFT

Robinson Carnes pilgrimmed along the country road between Sanderson and Elmville. He wore a shabby clerical suit, and he carried a rusty black bag which might have contained sermons. It did actually hold one sermon, a favorite which he had delivered many times in many pulpits, and in which he felt a certain covert pride of authorship.

The bag contained, besides the sermon, two old shirts with frayed cuffs, three collars, one pocket-handkerchief, a Bible, and a few ancient toilet articles. These were all his worldly goods, except the clothes he wore, and a matter of forty-odd cents in his old wallet. Robinson Carnes subsisted after a curious parasitical fashion. He travelled about the country with his rusty black bag, journeying from place to place — no matter what place, so long as it held an evangelical church. Straight to the parson of this church he went, stated his name and calling, produced certain vouchers in proof of the same, and inquired if he knew of any opening for a clergyman out of employment, if he had heard of any country pulpit in which an itinerant preacher might find humble harbor. He never obtained any permanent situation; he sometimes supplied a pulpit for a day, or officiated at a funeral or wedding, but that was all. But he never failed to receive hospitality, some sufficient meals, and lodging for one night at least in the parsonage guest-chamber.

Although Carnes's living was so precarious, he looked neither forlorn nor hungry. He had, in fact, had at noon an excellent dinner of roast beef at the home of the Presbyterian minister in Sanderson. It was the day before Christmas, and a certain subtle stir of festive significance was in the very air. Every now and then a wagon laden with young hemlocks, and trailing with greens passed him. The road was strewn with evergreen sprigs and stray branches, with an occasional jewel-like sprinkle of holly berries. Often he heard a silvery burst of laughter and chatter, and boys and girls appeared from a skirting wood with their arms laden with green vines and branches. He also met country carriages whose occupants had their laps heaped with parcels of Christmas presents. These last gave the tramp preacher a feeling of melancholy so intense that it amounted to pain. It was to him like the sight of a tavern to a drunkard when his pockets are empty and his thirst is great. It touched Robinson Carnes in his tenderest point. He had fallen a victim in early youth to a singular species of spiritual dissipation. Possessed by nature of a most unselfish love for his kind, and an involuntary generosity, this tendency, laudable in itself, had become in time like a flower run wild until it was a weed. His love of giving amounted to a pure and innocent but unruly passion. It had at one time assumed such proportions that it barely escaped being recognized as actual mania. As it was, people, even those who had benefited by his reckless generosity, spoke of him as a mild idiot.

There had been a day of plenty with him, for he had fallen joint heir to a large and reasonably profitable New England farm and a small sum in bank. The other heir was his younger brother. His brother had just married. Robinson told him to live on the farm and give him a small percentage of the profits yearly. When the crops failed through bad weather and mismanagement, he said easily, without the slightest sense of self-sacrifice, that the brother need not pay him the percentage that year. The brother did not pay it, as a matter of course, the next year, and in fact never did. In three years the brother's wife was ailing and the family increasing, and he was in debt for the taxes. Robinson paid them all, and he continued paying them as long as his money in the bank lasted. He wished his brother to keep his share intact, on account of his family. Then he gave from his poor salary to everything and everybody. Then he was in debt for his board. He rented a small room, and lived, it was said, on oatmeal porridge until the debt was paid.

Robinson Carnes had a fierce honesty. When he was in debt, he felt, for the first time in his life, disgraced, and like hiding his head. He often reflected with the greatest shame upon that period of his life when he had an impulse to go out of his way to avoid the woman whom he owed. He felt nothing like it now, although to some his present mode of existence might savor of beggary. He considered that in some fashion he generally rendered an equivalent for the hospitality which kept the breath of life in him. Sometimes the minister who entertained him was ailing, and he preached the sermon in his black bag in his stead. Sometimes he did some copying for him; often he had toiled to good purpose at his wood-pile or in his garden; he had even assisted the minister's wife with her carpet-beating in her spring cleaning. He had now nothing to be ashamed of, but he felt his very memory burn with shame when he remembered that time of debt. That had been the end of his career as a regularly settled minister. People might have forgiven the debt, but they could not forgive nor overlook the fact that while in such dire straits he had given away the only decent coat which he owned to wear in the pulpit, and also that he had given away to a needy family, swarming with half-fed children, the cakes and pies with which some female members of his parish had presented him to alleviate his oatmeal diet. That last had in reality decided the matter. He was requested to resign.

So Robinson Carnes resigned his pastorate, and had never been successful in obtaining another. He went out of the village on foot. He had given away every dollar of the last instalment of his meagre salary to a woman in sore straits. He had given away his trunk years ago to a young man about to be married and settle in the West. He regretted leaving his sermons behind because of the lack of a trunk. He stored them in a barrel in the garret of one of the deacon's houses. He stowed away what he could of his poor little possessions in his black bag, feeling thankful that no one had seemed to need that also. Since he had given away his best coat, he had only his old one, which was very shabby. When he shook hands with his half-hearted friends at parting, he was careful not to raise his right arm too high, lest he reveal a sad rip in the under-arm seam. Since, he had had several coats bestowed upon him by his clerical friends, when an old one was on the verge of total disruption, but the new coat was always at variance as to its right under-arm seams. Robinson Carnes had thereby acquired such an exceedingly cautious habit of extending his right arm as to give rise to frequent inquiries whether he had put his shoulder out of joint or had rheumatism. Now the ripped seam was concealed by an old but very respectable and warm overcoat which the Presbyterian minister in Sanderson had bestowed upon him, and which he had requited by an interpretation of the original Greek of one of the gospels, which aided the minister materially in the composition of his Christmas sermons. Carnes was an excellent Hebrew and Greek scholar, and his entertainer was rusty and had never been very proficient. Robinson had been in the theological seminary with this man, and had often come to his aid when there. Robinson had also set up the Christmas-tree for the Sunday-school in the church vestry. He was exceedingly skilful with his hands. The Christmas-tree had awakened in him the old passion, and his face saddened as he looked at the inviting spread of branches.

"I wish I had something to hang on the tree for your children and the Sunday-school," he said, wistfully, to the minister; and the other man, who knew his history, received his speech in meaning silence. But when Carnes repeated his remark, being anxious that his poor little gift of a Christmas wish, which was all that he had to offer, might at least be accepted, the other replied coldly that one's first duty was to one's self, and unjustified giving was pauperizing to the giver and the recipient.

Then poor Robinson Carnes, abashed, for he understood the purport of the speech, bade the minister good-by meekly and went his way. When he saw the other Christmas-trees on the road to Elmville, his wistful sadness became intensified. He felt the full bitterness of having absolutely nothing to give, of having even a kindly wish scorned when the wish was his last coin. He felt utterly bankrupt as to benefits towards his fellow-creatures, that sorest bankruptcy for him who can understand it.

Carnes had just watched a wagon loaded with Christmas greens pass slowly out of sight around a bend in the road, when he came unexpectedly upon a forlorn company. They were so forlorn, and so unusual in the heart of a prosperous State, that he could hardly believe his eyes at first. They seemed impossible. There were six of them in all: a man, two women — one young and one old — and three children: one a baby two years old, the others five and eight. The man stood bolt-upright, staring straight ahead with blank eyes; the women were seated on the low stone wall which bordered the road. The younger, the mother, held the five-year-old child; the older, evidently the grandmother, held the youngest; the eldest — all were girls — sat apart, huddled upon herself, her small back hooped, hugging herself with her thin arms in an effort to keep warm. As Carnes drew near she looked at him, and an impulse of flight was evident in her eyes. The younger of the two women surveyed him with a sort of apathy which partook of anger. The youngest child, in the old woman's lap, was wailing aloud. The grandmother did not try to hush it. Her face, full of a dumb appeal to and questioning of something which Carnes felt dimly was beyond him, gazed over the small head in a soiled white hood which beat wrathfully against her withered bosom. The woman wore an old shawl which was warm; she kept a corner well wrapped about the crying child. The younger woman was very thinly clad. Her hat had a pathetic last summer's rose in it. Now and then a long rigor of chill passed over her; at such times her meagre body seemed to elongate; her arms held the little girl on her lap like two clamps. The man, standing still, with face turned towards the sky over the distant horizon line, gave a glance at Carnes with eyes which bore no curiosity or interest, but were simply indifferent. He looked away again, and Carnes felt that he was forgotten, while his shadow and the man's still intermingled.

Then Carnes broke the silence. He stepped in front of the man. "See here, friend," he said, "what's the matter?"

The man looked at him perforce. He was past words. He had come to that pass where speech as a means of expression seemed superfluous. His look said as much to his questioner. "You ask me what is the matter?" the look said. "Are you *blind?*" But the question in the man's dull eyes was not resentful. He was not one in whom misery arouses resentment against others or Providence. Fate seemed to have paralyzed him, as the clutch of a carnivorous animal is said to paralyze a victim.

"What is it?" Carnes inquired again. "What is the matter?"

Still the man did not answer, but the younger of the two women did. She spoke with great force, but her lips were stiff, and apparently not a muscle of her face moved. "I'll tell you what the matter is," said she. "He's good for nothing. He's a no-account man. He ain't fit to take care of a family. That's what's the matter." Then the other woman bore her testimony, which was horrible from its intensity and its triviality. It was the tragedy of a pin-prick in a meagre soul.

"He's left my hair sofy an' my feather-bed," said she, in a high, shrill plaint.

Then the forlorn male, badgered betwixt the two females of his species, who were, as it often happens with birds, of a finer, fiercer sort than he, broke silence with a feeble note of expostulation. "Now, don't mother," said he. "You shall hev that sofy and that feather-bed agin."

The younger woman rose, setting the little girl on the frozen ground so hard that she began to cry. "Have 'em back? How is she goin' to have 'em back?" she demanded. "There's the hair-cloth sofy she earned and set her eyes by, and there's the feather-bed she's always slept on, left over there in Sanderson, stored away in a dirty old barn. How's she goin' to ever get 'em again? What's the poor old woman goin' to sit on an' sleep on?"

"We'll go back an' git 'em," muttered the man. "Don't, Emmy."

"Yes, I will! I'll tell the truth, and I don't care who knows it. You're a no-account man. How are we goin' to git 'em back, I'd like to know? You hain't a cent and you can't get work. If I was a man, I'd git work if it killed me. How is your mother goin' to git that sofy and feather-bed again as long as she lives? And that ain't all — there's all my nice furniture that I work for and earned before I was married; you didn't earn none of it except jest that one bedstead and bureau that you bought. I earned all the other things workin' in the shop myself, and there they all be stored in that dirty old barn to be eaten up by rats and covered with dust."

"We will get 'em back. Don't, Emmy."

"How'll you get 'em back? You're a good-for-nothin' man. You ain't fit to support a family."

"He's left my sofy an' feather-bed," reiterated the old woman.

The man looked helplessly from one to the other; then he cast a glance at Carnes — that look full of agony and appeal which one man gives another in such a crisis when he is set upon by those whom he cannot fight.

Carnes, when he met his fellow-man's piteous look, felt at once an impulse of partisanship. He stepped close to him and laid a hand on the thin shoulder in the thin coat. "See here, friend," he said, "tell me all about it." The compassion in Carnes's voice was a power in itself; he had, moreover, a great deal of the clergyman evident, as well in his manner as in the cut of his clothes.

The man hesitated a moment, then he began, and the story of his woes flowed like a stream. It was a simple story enough. The man was evidently one of those who work well and faithfully while in harness, like a horse. Taken out, he was naked and helpless and ashamed, without spirit enough to leave his old hitching-posts and beaten roads of life and gallop in new pastures unbridled. He became a poor nondescript, not knowing what he knew. The man, whose name was William Jarvis, had worked in a shoe factory ever since he was a boy. He had been an industrious and skilled workman, but had met with many vicissitudes. He had left a poor position for an exceedingly lucrative one in a large factory in Sanderson, and had moved there with his family. Then the factory had been closed through the bankruptcy of the owner. Since then he had had a hard time. He had left his family in Sanderson in their little rented house, and he had been about the country seeking in vain for employment. Then he had returned, to find that the old factory was to be reopened in a month's time, and then he could have a job; but every cent of his money was gone, and he was in debt. Not only Jarvis's money was gone, but his credit. The tradesmen had learned to be wary about trusting the shifting factory population.

The rent was due on the house; Jarvis paid that, and was literally penniless. He packed his humble furniture, and stored it in a neighbor's barn, on condition that it should be taken for storage if he did not claim it within a year.

Then he and his family set forth. It was the hopeless, senseless sort of exodus which might have been expected of people like these, who deal only with the present, being incapacitated, like some insects, from any but a limited vision in one direction. Carnes received a confused impression, from a confused statement of the man, that they had a hope of being able to reach a town in the northern part of the State, where the wife had some distant relatives, and the others of this poor clan might possibly come to their rescue. They had had a hope of friendly lifts in northward-journeying wagons. But there had been no lifts, and they had advanced only about five miles towards their forlorn Mecca on the day before Christmas. The children were unable to walk farther, and the parents were unable to carry them. The grandmother, too, was at the end of her strength. The weather was very cold, and snow threatened. They were none too warmly clad. They had only the small luggage which they could carry — an old valise, and a bundle tied up in an old shawl. The middle child had an old doll that had lost one arm, her blond wig, and an eye, but was going on her travels in her best, faded pink muslin dress and a bit of blue sash. The child stood sobbing wearily, but she still held fast to the doll. The eldest girl eyed her with tender solicitude. She had outgrown dolls. She got a dingy little handkerchief from her pocket and folded it cornerwise for a shawl; then she got down from the wall and pinned it closely around the doll. "There," she said, "that is better." After that the children themselves felt warmer.

Carnes saw everything — the people, the doll, their poor little possessions — and an agony of pity, which from the nature of the man and its futility became actual torture, seized him. He looked at the other man who had confided in him, at the women who now seemed to watch him with a lingering hope of assistance. He opened his mouth to speak, but he said nothing. What could he say?

Then the man, William Jarvis, added something to this poor story. Two weeks before he had slipped on the ice and injured his shoulder; he had strained it with moving, and it was causing him much distress. Indeed, his face, which was strained with pain as well as misery, bore witness to the truth of that.

The wife had eyed her husband with growing concentration during this last. When he had finished, her face brightened with tenderness; she made a sudden move forward and threw her arms around him, and began to weep in a sort of rage of pity and love and remorse. "Poor Willy! poor Willy!" she sobbed. "Here we've been abusin' you when you've worked like a dog with your shoulder 'most killin' you. You've always done the best you could.

I don't care who says you haven't. I'd like to hear anybody say you haven't. I guess they wouldn't darse say it twice to me." She turned on the old woman with unreasoning fury. "Hold your tongue about your old hair-cloth sofy an' your feather-bed, grandma!" said she. "Ain't he your own son? I guess you won't die if you lose your old hair-cloth sofy an' your feather-bed! The stuffin' all comin' out of your old sofy, anyhow! You'd ought to be ashamed of yourself, grandma! Ain't he your own son?"

"I guess he was my son afore he was your husband," returned the old woman, with spirit. "I ain't pesterin' of him any more'n you be, Emmy Jarvis." With that she began to weep shrilly like a child, leaning her face against the head of the crying child in her lap. The little girl with the doll set up a fresh pipe of woe; the doll slipped to the ground. The elder sister got down from the stone wall and gathered it up and fondled it. "You've dropped poor Angelina and hurt her, Nannie," said she, reproachfully.

"Poor Willy!" again sobbed his wife, "you've been treated like a dog by them you had a right to expect something better of, an' I don't care if I do say so."

Again the man's eyes, overlooking his wife's head, sought the other man's for an understanding of this peculiar masculine distress.

Carnes returned the look with such utter comprehension and perfect compassion as would have lifted the other's burden for all time could it have taken practical form. In reality, Carnes, at this juncture, suffered more than the man. Here was a whole family penniless, suffering. Here was a man with the impulse of a thousand Samaritans to bring succor, but positively helpless to lift a finger towards any alleviation of their misery. It became evident to him in a flash what the outside view of the situation would be: that the only course for a man of ordinary sense and reason was to return to Sanderson and notify the authorities of this suicidal venture; that it was his duty for the sake of the helpless children to have them cared for by force, if there was no other way. But still, this course he could not bring himself to follow. It seemed an infringement upon all the poor souls had left in the world — their individual freedom. He could not do it, and yet what else was there to do? He thought of his forty cents, his only available asset against this heavy arrear of pity and generosity, with fury. At that moment the philanthropist without resources, the Samaritan without his flask of oil, was fairly dangerous to himself from this terrible blocking of almost abnormal impulses for good. It seemed to him that he must die or go mad if he could not do something for these people. He cast about his eyes, like a drowning man, and he saw in a field on the left, quite a distance away, a small house; only its chimneys were visible above a gentle slope. A thought struck him. "Wait a moment," he ordered, and leaped the stone wall and ran across the field, crunching the frozen herbage until his footsteps echoed loudly. The forlorn family watched him. It was only a short time before he returned. He caught up the second little girl from the ground. "Come!" cried Carnes in an excited voice. "Come. Nobody lives in that house over there! I can get in! There is a shed with hay in it! There's a fireplace! There's plenty of wood to pick up in the grove behind it! Come!"

His tone was wild with elation. Here was something which could be done. It was small, but something. The others were moved by his enthusiasm. Their faces lightened. The father caught the youngest child from the grandmother; the mother took the eldest by the hand. They all started, the old grandmother outracing them with a quick, short-stepped toddle like a child. "See your mother go," said the wife, and she fairly laughed. In fact, the old woman was almost at her last gasp, and it was an extreme effort of nature, a final spurt of nerve and will.

The house was a substantial cottage, in fair repair. The door at the back was unlocked. Carnes threw it open and ushered in the people as if they had been his guests. A frightful chill struck them as they entered. It was much colder than outside, with a concentration of chill which overwhelmed like an actual presence of wintry death. The children, all except the eldest girl, who hugged the doll tightly, and whispered to her not to mind, it would be warm pretty soon, began to cry again. This was a new deprivation added to the old. They had expected something from the stranger, and he had betrayed them. The grandmother leaned exhausted against the wall; her lips moved, but nothing could be heard. The wife caught up the youngest crying child and shook her.

"Be still, will you?" she said, in a furious voice. "We've got enough to put up with without your bawling." Then she kissed and fondled it, and her own tears dropped fast on its wet face.

But not one whit of Carnes's enthusiasm abated. He beckoned the man, who sprang to his bidding. They brought wood from the grove behind the house. Carnes built a fire on the old hearth, and he found some old boxes in the little barn. He rigged up some seats with boards, and barrels for backs; he spread hay on the boards for cushions. The warmth and light of the fire filled the room. All of a sudden it was furnished and inhabited. Their faces began to relax and lighten. The awful blue tints of cold gave place to soft rose and white. The children began to laugh.

"What did I tell you?" the eldest girl asked the doll, and she danced it before the ruddy glow. The wife bade her husband sit with his lame shoulder next the fire. The youngest child climbed into her grandmother's lap again, and sat with her thumb in her mouth surveying the fire. She was hungry, but she sucked her own thumb, and she was warm. The old woman nodded peacefully. She had taken off her bonnet, and her white head gleamed with a rosy tint in the firelight.

Carnes was radiant for a few minutes. He stood surveying the transformation he had wrought. "Well, now, this is better," he said, and he laughed like a child. Then suddenly his face fell again. This was not a solution of the problem. He had simply stated it. There was no food, there was no permanent shelter. Then the second little girl, who was the most delicate and nervous of them all, began to cry again. "I want somefin to eat," she wailed. Her father, who had been watching them with as much delight as Carnes, also experienced a revulsion. Again he looked at Carnes.

"Yes," said the wife in a bitter tone, "here is a fire and a roof over us, but we may get turned out any minute, if anybody sees the smoke comin' out of the chimney; and there's nothin' to eat."

The eldest little girl's lip quivered. She hugged the doll more closely.

"Don't cry, and you shall have a piece of cake pretty soon," she whispered. The man continued to look at Carnes, who suddenly stood straight and threw up his head with a resolute look. "I'm going, but I will come back very soon," said he, "and then we'll have supper. Don't worry. Put enough wood on the fire to keep warm." Then he went out.

He hurried across the field to the road under the lowering quiet of the gray sky. His resolve was stanch, but his heart failed him. Again the agony of balked compassion was over him. He looked ahead over the reach of frozen highway without a traveller in sight, he looked up at the awful winter sky threatening with storm, and he was in a mood of blasphemy. There was that misery, there was he with the willingness to relieve, and — forty cents. It was a time when money reached a value beyond itself, when it represented the treasure of heaven. This poor forty cents would buy bread, at least, and a little milk. It would keep them alive a few hours, but that was only a part of the difficulty solved. The cold was intense, and they were not adequately protected against it. There were an old woman and three children. He was only giving them the most ephemeral aid, and what would come next?

Carnes, standing there in the road all alone, mechanically thrust his hand in his pocket for the feel of his forty cents; but instead of putting his hand in his own coat-pocket, he thrust it in the pocket of the overcoat which the minister in Sanderson had given him. He pulled out, instead of his own poor old wallet, a prosperous portly one of black seal-skin. He did not at first realize what it meant. He stood staring vacuously. Then he knew. The minister in Sanderson had left his own wallet in the overcoat pocket. The coat was one which he had been wearing until his new one had come from the tailor's the day before.

Carnes stood gazing at this pocket-book; then he slowly, with shaking fingers, opened it. There were papers, which he saw at a glance were valuable, and there was a large roll of bills. Carnes began counting them slowly. He sat down on the stone wall the while. His legs trembled so that he could scarcely stand. There was over two hundred dollars in bills in the wallet. Carnes sat awhile regarding the bills. A strange expression was coming over his gentle, scholarly, somewhat weak face — an expression evil and unworthy in its original meaning, but, as it were, glorified by the motive which actuated it. The man's face became full of a most angelic greed of money. He was thinking what he could do with only a hundred dollars of that other man's money. He knew with no hesitation that he would run to Elmville, hire a carriage, take the distressed family back to Sanderson to their old house, pay the rent a month in advance, pay their debts, get the stored furniture, help them set it up, give them money to buy fuel and provisions for the month before the factory opened. A hundred dollars of that money in his hand, which did not belong to him, meant respite for distress, which would be like a taste of heaven; it meant perhaps life instead of death; it meant perhaps more than earthly life, perhaps spiritual life, to save this family from the awful test of despair.

Carnes separated a hundred dollars from the rest. He put it in his own old wallet. He replaced the remainder in the minister's, and he went on to Elmville.

It was ten o'clock on Christmas-eve before Robinson Carnes, having left the Jarvis family reinstated in their old home, warmed and fed, and happier perhaps than they had ever been or perhaps ever would be, went to the vestry blazing with light in which the Christmas-tree was being held. He stood in the door and saw the minister, portly and smiling, seated well forward. As he watched, the minister's name was called, and he received a package. The minister was a man with a wealthy parish; he had, moreover, money of his own, and not a large reputation for giving. Carnes reflected upon this as he stood there. It seemed to him that with such a man his chances of mercy were small. He had his mind steeled for the worst. He considered, as he stood there, his very good chance of arraignment, of imprisonment. "It may mean State prison for me," he thought. Then a wave of happiness came over him. "Anyway," he told himself, "they have the money." He did not conceive of the possibility of the minister taking away the money from that poverty and distress; that was past his imagination. "They have the money," he kept repeating. It also occurred to him, for he was strong in the doctrines of his church creed, that he had possibly incurred a heavier than earthly justice for his deed; and then he told himself again, "Well, they have it."

A mental picture of the family in warmth and comfort in their home came before him, and while he reflected upon theft and its penalty, he smiled like an angel. Presently he called a little boy near by and sent him to the minister.

"Ask Mr. Abbott if he will please see Mr. Carnes a moment," he said. "Say he has something important to tell him."

Soon the boy returned, and his manner unconsciously aped Mr. Abbot.

"Mr. Abbot says he is sorry, but he cannot leave just now," he said. It was evident that the minister wished to shake off the mendicant of his holy profession.

Carnes took the rebuff meekly, but he bade the boy wait a moment. He took a pencil from his pocket and wrote something on a scrap of paper. He wrote this:

> "I found this wallet in your pocket in the coat which you gave me. I have stolen one hundred dollars to relieve the necessities of a poor family. I await your pleasure, Robinson Carnes."

The boy passed up the aisle with the pocket-book and the note. Carnes, watching, saw a sudden convulsive motion of the minister's shoulders in his direction, but he did not turn his head. His name was called again for a present as the boy passed down the aisle, returning to Carnes.

Again the boy unconsciously aped Mr. Abbot's manner as he addressed Carnes. It was conclusive, coldly disapproving, nonretaliative, dismissing. Carnes knew the minister, and he had no doubt. "Mr. Abbot says that he has no need to see you, that you can go when you wish," said the boy. Carnes knew that he was quite free, that no penalty would attach to his theft.

The snow had begun to fall as Robinson Carnes took his way out of Sanderson on the road to Elmville, but the earth had come into a sort of celestial atmosphere which obliterated the storm for human hearts. All around were innocent happiness and festivity, and the display of love by loving gifts. The poor minister was alone on a stormy road on Christmas eve. He had no presentiment of anything bright in his future: he did not know that he was to find an asylum and a friend for life in the clergyman in the town toward which his face was set. He travelled on, bending his shoulders before the sleety wind. His heart was heavier and heavier before the sense of his own guilt. He felt to the full that he had done a great wrong. He had stolen, and stolen from his benefactor. He had taken off the minister's coat and laid it gently over the back of a settee in the vestry before he left, but that made no difference. If only he had not stolen from the man who had given him his coat. And yet he always had, along with the remorse, that light of great joy which could not be wholly darkened by any thought of self, when he reflected upon the poor family who were happy. He thought that possibly the minister had in reality been glad, although he condemned him. He began to love him and thank him for his generosity. He pulled his thin coat closely around him and went on. He had given the last gift which he had to give — his own honesty.